THE FIRST AT THE BEACH ON D-DAY

a novel

Burt Jagolinzer

The First at the Beach on D-Day
Copyright © 2022 Burt Jagolinzer

Produced and printed by Stillwater River Publications.
All rights reserved. Written and produced in the
United States of America. This book may not be reproduced or
sold in any form without the expressed, written permission of the
author(s) and publisher.

Visit our website at
www.StillwaterPress.com
for more information.

First Stillwater River Publications Edition

ISBN: 978-1-958217-05-4

12345678910
Written by Burt Jagolinzer
Cover Art by Lindsay Whelan
Published by Stillwater River Publications,
Pawtucket, RI, USA.

*The views and opinions expressed
in this book are solely those of the author(s)
and do not necessarily reflect the views
and opinions of the publisher.*

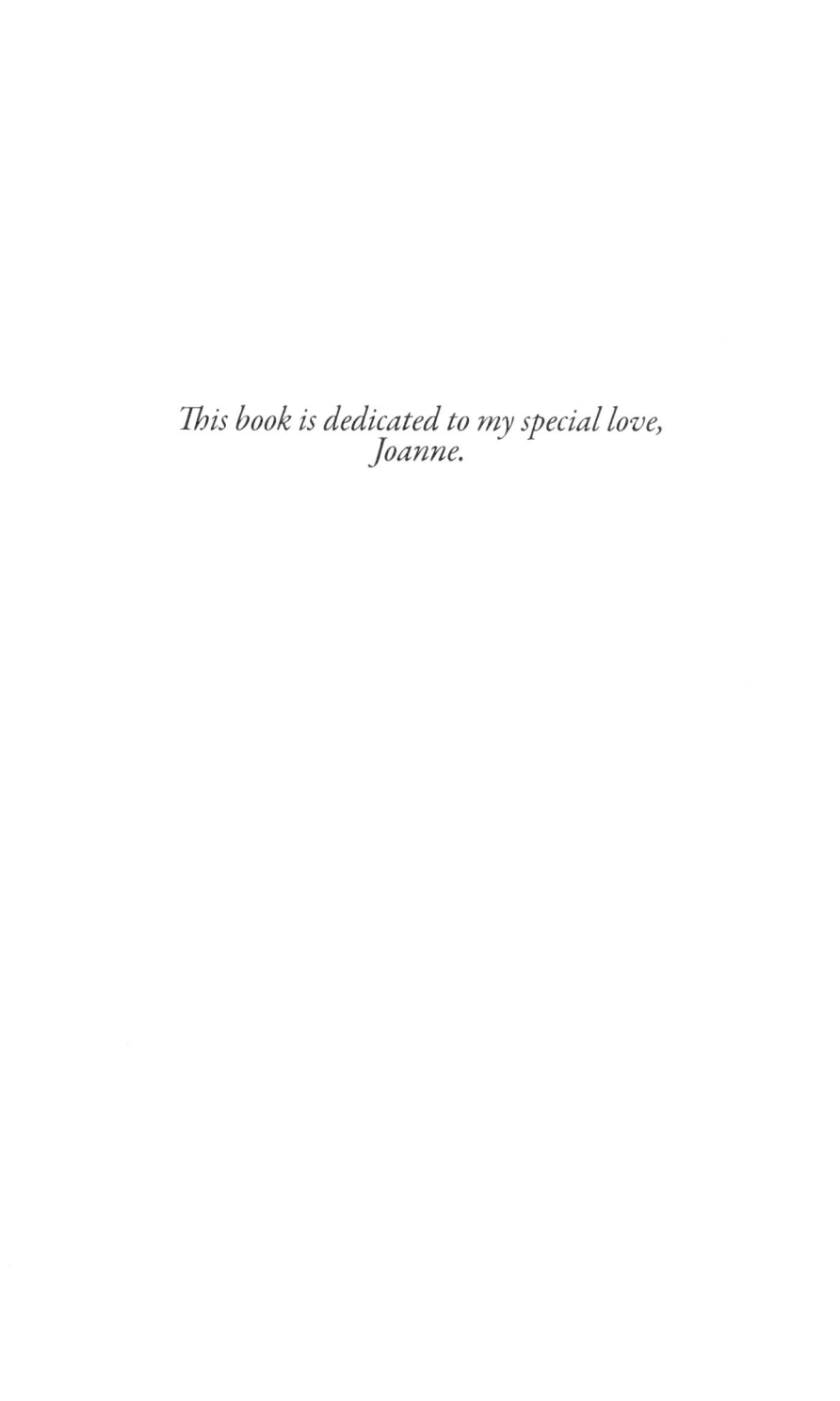

*This book is dedicated to my special love,
Joanne.*

THE FIRST AT THE BEACH ON D-DAY

ONE

ROBERT JOHN ("RJ") SMIDT was born in Heidelberg, Germany, on the 14th of February 1925.

RJ's father was a coal miner, and his mother cleaned homes.

His younger brother Boris left school at age thirteen and began work at a food market close to their home.

An older brother Otto was in a recovery home, recuperating from a terrible bout with typhoid fever.

RJ was finishing high school.

It was now January, 1941.

Adolph Hitler had taken complete control of Germany and had begun his forced expansion of several nearby countries.

Hitler had made a deal with Stalin of Russia to capture Poland and divide the conquered territory.

During RJ's last year in school, he was forced to pledge obedience and loyalty to only Hitler.

His parents knew that this was wrong. The Nazis had taken away his teacher, and he was believed to have been killed.

A new military instructor took over the classroom.

Also, at this time, the Nazis had begun total elimination of Jews, and anyone else that they felt objected or diverted their control of most everything.

The Nazis destroyed retirement homes, nursing homes and the like, killing all their individuals as well.

When RJ's family attempted to visit their son Otto, they were told that he had been relocated and would contact them later.

The Smidt family knew what the Nazis had done. It was the last straw. The Smidt family needed to escape Germany and in a hurry.

Fortunately, his mother's brother Oscar had moved to England several years prior, and a visit to England might give them a chance to leave their home and country.

It was not going to be easy.

TWO

GETTING VISAS was nearly impossible. You would need strong connections to even attempt such a feat.

The Nazis had tightened control of individuals leaving and coming into the country. They were preparing for large scale aggression, and they had secured their borders on all levels.

The Smidts, realizing the difficult situation, decided to attempt to send RJ to England by himself as a student in German History.

Maybe, if he succeeded, he could hopefully find a path to bring the rest of his family to Britain as well.

It appeared to be the only way, and even that would be difficult to achieve. But they were determined to try.

Because RJ had an aunt and uncle in London to house him, the German authorities saw no harm in approving his application.

He was to be given a twelve-month visa to study the world's views of German history when he was accepted at Cambridge Academy.

His passport and visa required RJ to return to Germany on the second day beyond the twelve months.

Attached to his passport was a formal letter, indicating that if RJ failed to return to Germany as agreed, his family members would face appropriate consequences.

After learning of the possible harm to his family, RJ didn't want to go. But his parents insisted that he go as offered and not to worry.

RJ began to pack. His train ticket had arrived.

He was to leave the day after tomorrow on a morning train.

THREE

RJ WOULD CERTAINLY visit his mother's brother Oscar if he was to have the chance.

He had met his uncle when he was about ten years old.

Uncle Oscar had visited their home in Heidelberg. He stayed for about three or four days.

His wife could not make the trip as she had been hospitalized for several serious problems.

Unfortunately, she passed away when his uncle returned home.

As far as they knew he was living alone and was quite old.

THE FIRST AT THE BEACH ON D-DAY

RJ was given his address and encouraged to visit him when possible.

FOUR

RJ THOUGHT the arrangement was too good. He was filled with doubt and concern.

The train ride to Calais, France was the first part of the trip. He was then to ferry across the English Channel to a port of entry into Great Britain.

From there he was to take a train or bus to Cambridge. If everything went right, it could be done in a complete day.

He had now boarded his first train. It was loaded with German soldiers and sailors, obviously heading in different directions.

RJ was given a seat next to a Wehrmacht soldier, barely a teenager.

The soldier offered him a cigarette. Not being a smoker, RJ refused the kind offer.

"Where are you going?" the soldier asked.

"I am going to school . . . in Britain," RJ responded.

"We will be conquering England soon, and you will be killed," he blabbed. "Why would a German go to England at this time to study?"

"Our government is anxious to learn what England might think of us, at this time. I will return in a year, to my awaiting family," RJ answered.

There was silence.

The door to their train compartment was opened. There stood a ranking military officer. He demanded passports and papers.

RJ's papers didn't seem to make sense to the officer.

He said abruptly, "I will return quite quickly," and he disappeared.

Minutes later the officer returned with a higher ranking official.

"Why would our government send you to our enemy?" he shouted.

"I am a history major, and they want me to boast of our wonderful country and its ancient history. They also want me to return with information on how they envision our current political situation, etc. I will report directly to Berlin or others to be assigned," RJ returned.

"Very good. We must be very careful who is to leave our country, as well as who comes into it," the official ended, and saluted him.

The train made its way close to the French border and stopped.

Most of the individuals and soldiers were to leave the train at this point and disperse in many other directions.

Maybe a dozen soldiers and a few travelers remained on the train.

The train continued on to the French border. French soldiers boarded the train.

New passport checks and papers were readied for inspection.

The train was permitted to enter France and headed for Calais.

FIVE

THE GERMANS had already controlled the coming-and-going from that part of France.

Calais had become a vital point in the plans to conquer Great Britain, and it was deemed very important for U-Boat activity throughout the waters leading supplies to England.

The U-Boats were destroying ships headed to helping Britain survive the air attacks from the German Luftwaffe.

RJ's papers were checked and rechecked several times before boarding a small Swedish fishing boat authorized by the French authorities, which was promised to stop somewhere in a British harbor to deliver RJ.

He boarded the ship quickly and saluted the French Officers who had honored his credentials.

The small craft puttered its way across the English Channel to a place called Dover.

RJ was more than pleased to get off the boat, as the ride across was quite terrible. The wind and some rain caused great discomfort, and his clothes had become soaked.

Two British soldiers welcomed him to their country.

Once again, his papers were checked and rechecked by the soldiers.

He was then permitted to be driven to a bus connection that would bring him into greater London.

By mid-afternoon he had reached downtown London.

He was taken by the destruction of buildings and streets in the area.

There was a large cathedral, having taken a massive hit, and was still on fire. Hundreds of firemen and volunteers were rushing in several directions.

RJ knew that the German Air Force had been bombing special targets quite regularly and that Hitler had hoped that Britain would surrender.

At the London Commerce Building he was to meet Peter Kingsboro from the Cambridge Academy.

When he reached the Commerce Building, he was to ask for Peter.

Sure enough, Peter was waiting at tea within the building.

Peter insisted RJ sit at tea with him and get to know each other.

With his typical broad British accent, he began telling of his background to RJ.

Peter was a history professor at Cambridge Academy for nearly twelve years. He had studied at Oxford and received a degree in ancient and modern history.

Peter was thirty-four years old, married with two daughters, age eight and seven.

SIX

PETER SPOKE CLEARLY in the German language so that RJ could completely understand him.

RJ started giving his young life story to Peter, finishing with his unhappiness toward the Hitler controlled discrimination laws.

He also mentioned his brother's disappearance and how his family received the undocumented news that they had murdered him, and all others at the many retirement and health centers throughout Germany.

RJ went on to mention how his family wanted to immediately leave Germany but found it nearly impossible, and that he was picked by his mother to attempt to use his history skills to escape.

They had hoped that if he could get out of the country, that he could find a way to extract the remaining family members.

Peter understood his story and goals. He immediately responded, "We will hopefully help you in your important task."

They shook hands and left the tea setting, heading for Cambridge Academy, which had offered to welcome him, for an historic interchange.

Peter's 1937 Morris, Sedan automobile rambled along the back roads of rural London, heading for Cambridge.

Soon they arrived at the Academy proper.

RJ was taken to Perkins Hall, where he was given a small but comfortable room on the second floor, with a window overlooking a piece of the campus just below him.

Peter told him, "You will be picked-up at 7 AM and brought to my office for some breakfast before meeting my staff."

RJ thanked him for meeting him and bringing him this far and finished by saying "Good night" in English.

The trip from Germany to England had been completed.

"Thank God it was without major incident," RJ told himself.

SEVEN

THE NEXT MORNING, after meeting with Peter and enjoying his breakfast array of crumpets and juice followed by good coffee with fresh milk, RJ was brought to a lecture hall, where a full capacity seating of about four hundred students and faculty awaited his arrival speech in the German language.

However, to their surprise, RJ began his speech in rather perfect English.

"My country is in turmoil, as the government is now controlled by Heir Hitler and his murderers.

"They are destroying people, particularly Jews and educators. They are taking complete authority for everything that happens in the country without apology.

"My brother, who was in a rehabilitation center, was taken away with all the others and is believed to have been killed.

"The Gestapo has done the same to all retirement occupants as well as those in nursing homes and hospitals.

"Money that is being saved by the government by eliminating these helpless people is now being spent on military items, for Hitler's goal of conquering the world.

"My parents and I want to escape Germany, which is impossible to do now.

"But my parents had me apply for this historical scholarship knowing that the government wanted to know more about the conditions here in England. They have invested in me to report to them when I return.

"I am to return in twelve months, or else they will hurt my parents.

"My family does not want me to leave the freedom of England and say they will face the consequences if necessary.

"I don't want them to suffer any punishment because of my actions here.

"If there are ways to get my parents out of Germany, I must consider all possibilities.

"I cannot wait until my twelve months are completed.

"Military people speak regularly of conquering Great Britain.

"I hope that England can be ready to stop them. How and when they plan to overtake this country, I do not know.

"But, for this freedom that you and now I enjoy, I will do my part to help keeping it from Germany control.

"While here, I was committed to teaching European history, which is my formal education, and 1 will continue to apply that commitment.

"I look forward to that opportunity.

"Thank you for your cooperation on this matter."

Everyone in the hall stood up and applauded his speech.

RJ returned, with Peter, to his office.

Waiting there was fresh tea and finger cookies.

They sat and enjoyed the collation.

EIGHT

PETER HAD PROMISED RJ that he would investigate with the proper authorities if anything could be done to help his parents to escape Germany.

With that encouragement RJ believed that Peter's effort might just be the only chance he would have to help his family.

Meanwhile he was in safe England and must continue his teaching role that had been put upon him.

Cambridge Academy was an excellent school, with highly rated instructors and a student body of fortunate individuals from many countries.

He quickly realized that a reasonable number of these students would soon be called upon to serve in the military in the spreading war being promoted by his own country.

"I must help them in any way to prepare for war, which is about to reach all of Europe," RJ told himself.

"Peter will surely understand my position, and make use of my personal goals," he continued.

Indeed, Peter understood RJ's goals and began to implement his unusual offering.

He encouraged RJ to include in his everyday classroom teachings words that might enlighten his students on approaching war situations.

RJ's two classes per day included his reminder of the conditions in Germany, and how Heir Hitler's ultimate goal is to conquer and rule the world.

"His bombing of England is only the beginning. Hitler expects Britain to surrender. We must never surrender to his scares. Prepare to fight on in anyway possible," RJ added to each class recitals.

Sure enough, the air bombing continued almost every night. The destruction kept getting worse.

Expectations of an all-out attack from Germany frighten all of England.

The air raids showed no signs of stopping.

Behind the scenes Britain and the Allies had begun planning for various retaliations.

NINE

RJ WAS ESCORTED to his Uncle Oscar's home in the London suburb.

Professor Peter Kingsboro had offered to bring him to his aging uncle.

Peter waited outside his simple cottage.

The cottage had taken a bomb during a raid several months ago. It had destroyed an end room of the dwelling and completely eliminated the garage and neighboring buildings.

Fortunately, his uncle had not been touched during the attack.

Uncle Oscar was nearing eighty years old and had been a survivor of World War I. He had been in the battle at Belgium.

His right leg had received much shrapnel and he walked with a limp.

Oscar had received a note from a French soldier, who was stationed in "Free France," several days ago.

(Although the Nazi had taken a great portion of France, at that time, a portion was still considered neutral and was to eventually become occupied as well.)

The note had been smuggled out by a Belgian letter carrier, addressed to Oscar.

The letter, written in German, was from his sister, RJ's mother, announcing that they had been moved by the military to a camp. Their home had been destroyed during the Allies' air bombings.

She insisted that RJ not return to Germany.

"We don't know our future, but it is in their hands."

She wrote that RJ's return would not make any difference, and he would probably be inducted into the military to fight against freedom.

"Please tell RJ to stay in England and to fight for freedom.

"If we survive this war, we will surely attempt to meet up with all our family once again.

"Our heartfelt love to you, Oscar, and to our son, RJ if it becomes possible.

"Signed, your sister Beatrice."

RJ now knew his plans to return must be eliminated.

And so, he could now consider several other alternatives.

When he completed his teaching at Cambridge Academy he would decide exactly what direction to take.

Meanwhile he would discuss with Peter, and others, the several considerations.

He hugged his Uncle Oscar and left with the note in his hands.

The ride back to Cambridge Academy was sadly conversed. He now must worry about his parents.

The thought of never seeing his parents again was overtaking him.

TEN

THE GERMAN LUFTWAFFE continued to bomb England. Most of downtown London was surviving underground.

Although major damage was occurring throughout the Empire, the people were not about to give up. They would continue to produce vital equipment and supplies for the war.

Prime Minister Winston Churchill had promised his nation "To fight to the end, even if attacked on land."

Cambridge Academy had taken a small hit in its research laboratory.

Students were beginning to leave. Many would enlist in the Army.

Peter, because of his family, couldn't go to war.

RJ now considered entering the military as a German language aide.

Maybe they could find an important use for him, he thought.

He decided to approach the military to see what they would think.

Two days later, he was sent a special letter inviting him to a meeting at Thornton-Command in downtown London the very next day at 1300 hours.

RJ was prepared to go to that meeting.

ELEVEN

IT WAS 12:58 PM and RJ sat down in the office of Staff Corporal Arnold Reisen, head of special appointments for the British Army.

RJ began telling the corporal of his background and about his current stay in Britain.

The corporal was impressed by RJ's ability to speak fluently in at least two languages. He also accepted his overall story connecting himself to Cambridge Academy.

"Will you be willing to offer your services to our fight against your own country?" the corporal quizzed.

"Yes, my country is under the control of murderers, thieves, and world seekers, while torturing the people and countries they have conquered.

"I desperately want to pay back those who killed my brother, friends, and other family members. I want to help stop them and will do whatever I can to help make that happen.

"Please assign me to an important role to help England and the Allies win this war upon us," RJ countered.

"Go have some tea downstairs and return in about an hour," the Corporal responded.

RJ left the office, heading downstairs to the awaiting tea.

TWELVE

RJ RETURNED to the office.

Staff Corporal Arnold Reisen was waiting for him.

"I have discussed a series of possible important positions that you might be qualified to help us perform.

"They are checking out your background. When and if you receive clearance from our security division, we would be able to advance to the first of several steps that you have to take.

"I am expecting a report within the next twenty-four hours, to hopefully begin the process. Please contact me tomorrow at 1300 hours," he ended.

RJ immediately thanked the Corporal and left the building.

He headed back to Cambridge Academy.

Peter was there to meet him. "I hope that you have located the connections that you had sought?"

RJ responded, "Yes, I am being considered for important work for the war effort. I should know tomorrow whether they are accepting me.

"I need to get some sleep. I haven't been able to sleep the last two nights because of the bombing. Please excuse me now. I'll talk to you tomorrow morning. Thank you for your personal interest."

RJ went to his small apartment and quickly undressed, washed, and worked his way into bed.

THIRTEEN

RJ RECEIVED the call at 11:45 AM from the corporal. He sounded quite happy to report:

"You have been partially cleared, but not all checks are completed. Yet, I was given the go-ahead by the upper command to begin your processing.

"First, you must volunteer for enlistment, and be sworn-in to the British Army as a lance corporal. The swearing-in will take place tomorrow at 1400 hours in my office, if it is convenient for you.

"If all security checks out and you are approved, and your processing with me goes well, you will be a candidate for special duty that could award you a promotion to second lieutenant—which is required for unique assignment or assignments, at this time, which are being planned for you.

"The timing is right for someone like you, as the war continues to escalate. Our people are truly in need of your services. Your work could be very important in our future military movements.

"I look forward to your arrival tomorrow.

"If you have questions, we will attempt to answer them at this next meeting. Goodbye for now," he ended.

"Thank you, corporal. I will be with you tomorrow." RJ responded.

The bombing of London and surrounding areas continued as RJ attempted to catch up on his sleep.

FOURTEEN

YES, RJ arrived at the military office and was sworn into the British Army as a lance corporal.

He vowed to give his life, if necessary, to help defeat fascism and to play an assigned role in bringing this war to an end.

The first lieutenant who had led the formal induction congratulated RJ and softly welcomed him into the military service.

He announced that his next step would be to complete an abbreviated general induction class that normally would take a full week. RJ would be limited to only two days of this class.

Next, he was to be briefed in two more languages: French and Spanish.

He was given three days to convince training instructors of his ability to hold basic conversation in both speaking and writing.

Continuing, they sent him by train to an unknown location, far from London, heading towards Wales. (It was a special secret base, not known to many, for covert training.)

There he was quickly given exposure to signaling, coding, and delicate reconnaissance.

His training included wireless schooling and available explosive options.

RJ was then sent to an air training site and was taught parachute usage. He was finally sent up in an airplane for an air drop experience.

Next, he was sent to a field range for weapons training. It included small handguns, rifles, grenades, and several newly available firearms.

Having passed all of this quick training, he was given orders to report to a building in downtown London, which was unmarked and guarded by army soldiers.

His orders permitted RJ's entrance to the building. He was directed to the basement office.

There, he was to meet with British Lancer specialists.

They were expecting him.

He was escorted into a private room adjacent to the office entrance.

Six military men and one military woman were seated at a conference table, waiting for RJ's arrival.

The door was closed and locked. It was a well-lit room with maps and tables holding important information.

RJ was told to sit down at the end of the large table.

He was about to get his assignment and the background needed to begin his unknown role.

FIFTEEN

CAPTAIN OSCAR HAMM began with background. "You have been carefully chosen from a group of candidates.

"It is your German background that totally interested us, and was, more or less, the reason we picked you over the others.

"Now, with your recent training, we believe you should be quite qualified for some very important work that we are faced with.

"This is to be a completely secret program and we demand your guarantee not to converse, insinuate, or mention, in any manner, the program, your role, and or any connection to its implementation whatsoever.

"You have convinced your previous contacts of your firm desire to fight against the fascism of the Nazi regime, even to give your life if necessary.

"We have been told of what your family has endured and of the losses among your family, friends, and many others prior to coming to our country.

"Obviously, you have been aware of the bombing raids that they continue to bring to our homeland, and we are taking the punishment now to be repaid someday soon.

"The prime minister and the military leaders have assigned us, this committee, to help destroy their means and supplies that currently spearhead their forward movement to conquer Europe and the rest of the world.

"To this end, we have researched the enemy's logistical locations and have begun to sabotage key priority spots that have already affected certain war products that they have needed.

"It is now imperative that we continue to attack their crucial locations, hoping to stop their advancements all together.

"Our underground has been working quite well with the French Resistance in Occupied France.

"They have begged us for more help. We have been getting weapons and explosives to them for nearly three years.

"The resistance needs location data and information vital for their continual effect.

"Radio transmissions are picked up by the enemy and cannot be used any more.

"We must continue to feed the resistance updated information.

"Unfortunately, we can only do it by personal contact.

"The risk is quite high, but we have no alternate choices.

"You will be expected to be a carrier, to be dropped behind enemy lines, hopefully, to awaiting resistance individuals with that vital information for them.

"Major Sandra Darling will work with you over the details. She will prepare you for your role in this program.

"The major has been involved in our on-going research and events since our committee was formed several years ago.

"She is highly qualified to prepare you.

"You are to meet with her tomorrow at 0800 hours here.

"There will be tea and crumpets here for you both at that hour.

"Any questions about the program should be issued to her tomorrow.

"We are through with you for now.

"Our committee wishes you the very best of luck. Your effort in this program could save unknown quantities of lives, not just in France, but throughout Europe and elsewhere.

"Good hunting."

RJ left the room, saluting all the officers.

He was driven back to the academy, where Peter was waiting.

SIXTEEN

MAJOR SANDRA DARLING was a twenty-three-year-old native of Birmingham, England.

She was quite beautiful, with dirty-blonde hair parted to one side.

Her face, eyes, nose, and mouth truly indicated her youth. Yet, she was a veteran army officer who had already paid her dues in the military.

At nineteen she volunteered for the army, having lost her father in military training, prior to the beginning of the war.

Also, she had left a four year romantic affair when she found him on a weekend get-away with another woman.

In high school she had excelled in languages, speaking fluently in German, Spanish, and French.

At that time, the British Air Force needed to know the ever-changing locations of German airports, expecting possible trouble with Hitler's rising military power.

Sandra offered to go to Germany and obtain their current locations.

To do so, they immediately promoted her to the officer status of lieutenant.

Within a year she located and documented fourteen known air bases throughout most of Germany.

She was able to do it as a visitor on vacation and returned to England with this vital information.

Lieutenant Sandra Darling spent the next six months feeding air force leadership valuable information that had already become important for future strategy.

Soon, she was elevated to major.

The army selected her for this important committee, knowing well her background and skills.

She was living at home in Birmingham, with her widowed mother Irene.

The major quickly dressed in her military uniform at 0600 hours to drive to downtown London to meet with Lance-Corporal RJ Smidt.

It began to rain in most of England.

SEVENTEEN

RJ REACHED INTO his pocket to show the guards his initial orders, allowing him to enter the secret building once again.

He immediately returned to the room downstairs.

Major Sandra Darling was waiting for him. She arose from her desk and went to lock the door behind RJ.

He sat down facing her at the left end of the long conference table.

RJ was surprised to see that only the two of them were present.

His first thought was how attractive this Major was. He had not really noticed her among the group meeting of yesterday. It had been only a quick glance.

He could tell that she was somewhere near his age. But he had not gone further to investigate her.

It was now quite different. This attractive officer was about to teach him important procedures and maybe more.

"Welcome aboard," the major offered.

"Thank you. I look forward to your help regarding my special endeavors." RJ responded.

"Good. As you know I have a background in research and military movement that should be helpful to your plans.

"I had been instructed by command to introduce you to your first objective.

"Are you ready to receive this information?" she stated.

"Yes, I am in your hands, he replied.

"Okay. We have been apprised by intelligence that Germany's Tiger Tank, currently at forty-three tons, often called the Panzer, is now quite superior to any tank that is available to us or our Allies.

"Further, we now know that they are developing a new version called the Tiger-II, expected to be built with sixty-eight tons.

"We have been working on improved production of tanks that should hopefully compete with them.

"However, we have been told that our new tanks could be many months from reaching our front lines.

"Our research has located the two production plants, one in Germany and another in Austria. The air force has been notified and they are beginning to assign targets to destroy those factories.

"Needless to say, occupied France has several hundred of their tanks, and we are called upon to do anything and everything possible to slow them down and or eliminate them.

"Many are being transported from Germany to potential areas by trains.

"The resistance has destroyed some at the rails and continues guarding important areas, expected to be receiving their tanks.

"Our intelligence has received information that the resistance needs to know.

"Some of the information could save many lives.

"Also, we have a list of supply locations which is believed to be housing ammunition, fuel, and weapons that could be sabotaged.

"Our committee believes that if you were dropped behind enemy lines to the resistance, that you could accomplish what we consider 'vital' at this time.

"I am to go over the possible plan and the particulars with you.

"Please hold your questions until I am finished.

"But for now let's enjoy the tea and crumpets that has been given to us."

She began unbuttoning her outer uniform jacket. RJ followed with his jacket.

There was heat in the room, and too much of it.

EIGHTEEN

THE MAJOR BEGAN, "I don't believe this: six crumpets, boiled water, and just one tea bag. I guess we'll share the one bag, huh?"

"My, you are not only quite military, but also beautiful, and even a polite humorist. I wasn't sure that it would be possible.

"But I am delighted that, in your speech, you bring out a connection to our common ages.

"I would imagine that you know my background from the research that has been done of me, yes?" the lance-corporal replied.

"It is true. I do know your history and I have great sympathy for your family and you. And I do know why you have volunteered for this kind of assignment.

"Please, let us be friends. I am committed to spending the next two days with you, going over all kinds of possibilities that you could encounter on your mission.

"You seem like a nice guy and I can easily get emotionally attached to your objectives and even you.

"Let's drink some tea. The bag is yours first." Laughing, with a perfect smile, she handed him the tea bag.

They smiled at each other while imbibing the warm tea and crumpets.

After returning to their seats the major began once again. "You are to be taken by aircraft to a special location in occupied France, where you will be expected to parachute to awaiting contacts.

"You will be carrying important data and some supplies. Other chutes will be following you carrying explosives and sundry needs.

"A welcoming code word will guarantee your connection to the resistance. We must be sure that you will be dealing with the proper leaders.

"Hopefully, your contacts will bring you to a resistance gathering where you can trust releasing your special vital information.

"They should be grateful for all of the supplies that came with you.

"You will then begin to locate the explosive material that was dropped.

"Your training should easily lead you to carefully put together these new explosives, ready for detonation.

"The resistance should be anxious to use these explosives for effective use in stopping the Nazi advancements.

"Your up-to-date maps will help them accomplish these objectives.

"You may or may not be required to be with them on these particular actions. But you must be prepared to help them if they are not confident to do them alone.

"We will be expecting you to be with them no longer than a week.

"Then they will attempt to get you out of occupied France."

NINETEEN

THE MAJOR continued, "You will be dressed as a French peasant, with credentials identifying yourself as Jock LePare, a railroad engineer who studied at the Berlin Railroad School two years ago, and you have been traveling by various autos, stopping in small villages along the way, attempting to find your Aunt Belle, who has disappeared from her home in Calais.

"Your bag will be packed with simple clothes and one pair of shoes, toiletries, a flashlight, two batteries, and a small camera with film in it.

"Obviously, you are not to be caught with the camera or extra batteries, which are not allowed by the Nazi regulations. You could be tortured or even killed, if found with these items.

"You will be given some French currency and a German coin that could become valuable if stopped by the enemy.

"The resistance should provide you with food and sustenance while in their company.

"You are to get reasonable sleep throughout, while being aware of the limited securities about you.

"If the Nazis spot your drop in any way, they will be searching for you. It will make your objectives more difficult.

"But the resistance is used to it and will do their best to hide you and your supplies. You will have to trust them without choice.

"If you are caught, you must never give your real name nor background information. You are encouraged to use your language ability to work your way out of being detained or worse.

"No other information is to be given under any circumstance. Remember, you are to protect many lives that could be at stake.

"If you should be captured and sent to a camp, we advise you to seek other top leadership within your camp and eventually release your background, skills, and information. It could be helpful to others and even towards the possibility of escape planning, etc.

"Never try to reach us. We would be forced to deny any connection to you or our program.

"We will be waiting at our end for a notification from free French people of your arrival there.

"A transit to leave free France will already be issued and in the hands of the proper individuals who will be anxious to help you leave the area.

"We will be waiting for your safe return to London, hopefully having completed your mission and with stories and information important to our command.

"And, of course, I will be waiting as well."

TWENTY

"YOU WILL HAVE several sundry items in your jacket lining, and others in your backpack."

"In your lining will be two chocolate bars and a small wine container.

"Your backpack will carry a French canteen with water, a ham sandwich, and two homemade cookies. Also included will be a small, used pocketknife.

"Your maps and coded information will be carefully placed in your socks.

"One package of French cigarettes is being procured for you and it is to give to the resistance.

"Are you with me, at this stage?"

"Yes, I have one major question that hopefully you could answer.

"Can you obtain some sort of a French railroad badge that might help justify my fake skills?" RJ stated.

"I will request immediately a badge of some sort for you. I will also ask for a chance to teach you some basic train skills that could help you if needed.

"It may take a few days. We must be patient, as our professional printers work on our request.

"Meanwhile, I am sure someone will quickly organize some special time with train information for you to at least recognize and digest.

"Do you have any other pertinent questions that I might answer?" asked the major, ending her reply.

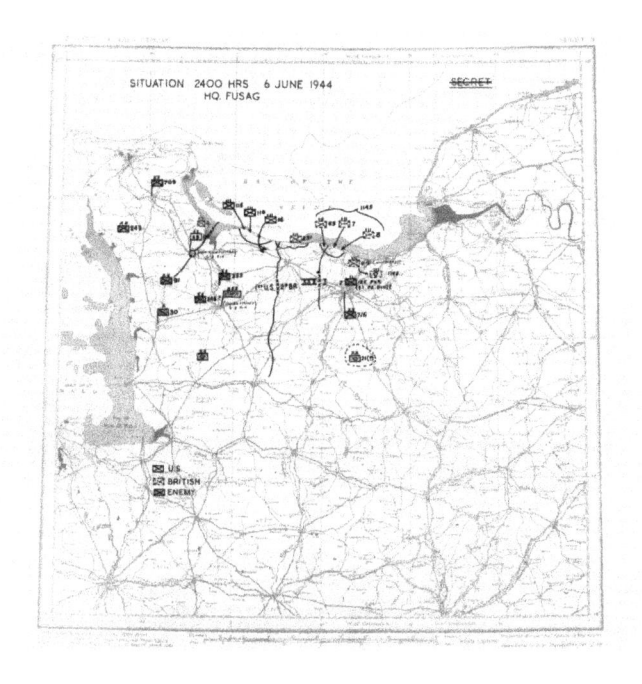

"No, but I would really want to get to know you better, if that is possible?" RJ countered.

"Yes, that would be alright. What did you have in mind?"

"How about lunch, I'm starving? Just anywhere is fine with me," RJ returned.

"Let's stay in uniform and we can go for lunch at the military cafe, about three blocks from here. We can even walk to the building," the major returned again.

They put their jackets back on and unlocked the door.

The walk was more like five blocks, but their conversation made it seem like only two.

His excellent manners led her to their seats, where he pulled back her chair and waited properly for her seating.

She thanked him for the courtesy, and they began to order their menu favorites.

Major Sandra made it clear that she had a budget for the lunch, and for him to just enjoy the collation.

TWENTY-ONE

THEY REMAINED at lunch for several hours.

Yes, they were getting to know each other.

The major asked, "Are you sure you want to carry out this mission? You realize that you may never return to England. Also, you might get killed, captured, tortured, wounded, or even dismembered.

"Remember, I'm getting to know you more each hour and I—along with the resistance—will be anxiously awaiting word of your return.

"Needless to say, you are beginning to see the importance of your proposed mission. It could have a great bearing on the movement of the war.

"It is truly a lot to put onto your shoulder. Just how do you feel about it?"

RJ responded, "What the Nazis have done to my family and country is unbelieveable. Remember, I have been there to see it happening right before my own eyes.

"I cannot stand by and watch their airplanes bomb England, run all over Europe, and threaten the remaining parts of the world.

"If I can help the resistance do their part in occupied France, to hold back the Nazi's advancements, then it will be worth it all.

"I note your personal concern for me in your remarks. I hope that it might mean a spark between us.

"Correct me if I'm wrong, but I detect a chemistry developing, yes?"

Major Sandra Darling returned, "Yes, I am truly getting to know you and it is favorable.

"At this point, we cannot push the military goals of our meeting into the background.

But maybe a relationship could develop.

"As in most war-time relationships it is best to be concerned about the future, but with a realistic question mark for survival.

"On that basis, I cannot look too hard at the future right now. I trust you would understand, yes?"

Corporal RJ answered, "Of course I understand. But I know that I'm attracted to you, by your beauty, manner of speech, and your soft and sincere method of working with me, and for me.

"I suspect you have gotten a personal feeling for me, yes?"

The major responded, "Yes, I see you as special. I like your looks, smile, and honesty. You are probably the nicest guy that I have met while in the service.

"But, as I have said, I cannot go further, because of the uncertainty of this war.

"I will continue to prepare you for the mission and pray for your safe return to us here in England.

"Please accept this answer. Let's return to the training facility."

TWENTY-TWO

THEY SPENT the afternoon back in the room.

Major Sandra Darling had relaxed and was beginning to treat RJ even more loosely, dropping most of the formal military approaches.

It became truly Sandra to RJ.

She had a message on her phone.

They had located a badge that was being touched up, indicating his attachment to the Berlin Railroad School. And he was to be exposed to the working of a typical train tomorrow.

They want him to be picked up at the Academy at 0800 hours.

"Could we meet up tomorrow night for dinner?" he asked

"I don't see why not. How about at Dowton's Cafe, just three streets over from here, about 1800 hours?" she responded.

They finished the afternoon talking about maps that could be very important to the French resistance.

Each map had come from reputable spies, scattered throughout occupied France.

Military people believed that these maps could help target additional important Nazi locations that would become possible sabotage priorities that will affect their movement.

RJ absorbed the statements being presented to him.

He now knew, more than ever, the real importance to his mission.

Major Sandra reached a point that wrapped up her requested work for today.

She wanted to know how he was doing. "Have we thrown too much at you for this long day?" she continued.

"I believe I have it all. I would rather spend whatever time is left just with you, if that is possible?" he begged.

"Yes, let's continue to get to know each other" she returned.

They spend nearly three more hours at the table.

She needed to take a bus to her home, and he needed to find a taxi for himself.

They rose from their chairs, reached across the table grabbing hands, and then RJ came around the corner and planted a soft meaningful kiss upon her waiting lips.

They left the building holding hands, said their goodbyes, and went their separate ways.

TWENTY-THREE

HE WAS TAKEN to a rail yard not far from the Academy.

Part of the yard had been demolished from previous bombings. Two engines were still workable.

Captain Wainwright escorted RJ into one of the workable engine compartments.

He was a veteran engineer who was working with the military on rail operations.

His knowledge was quite up-to-date so to speak. With his heavy British accent, he pointed to the general operations of the engine room, its normal procedures and faults.

After loading the furnace with some available wood, he started up the engine. He made it look quite easy.

RJ listened closely and asked key questions that could be important during a possible interrogation.

He was beginning to feel better about this part of the mission.

By noon, the captain had covered all concepts that he was instructed to go through with the corporal.

"Let's get some grub, as the American's call it," he shouted.

They spent nearly three hours at a local pub where the soup and sandwiches were quite delightful.

RJ would not imbibe liquor of any kind. The captain more than made up for it.

Finally, the captain drove him back to the academy. Most of the day had gone by.

RJ would take a short nap and then wash and dress for his dinner date with Major Sandra.

He was certainly looking forward to being with this attractive military lady who had just entered his life.

His thoughts brought him to wonder what she must be thinking about the dinner meeting and what might follow.

Resting on his bed, he closed his eyes and faded into dreamland.

Sure enough, about an hour later he arose from his needed nap and began to wash and dress.

He was certain that this evening's meeting would bring him closer to this desirable female, Major Sandra Darling.

TWENTY-FOUR

MAJOR SANDRA DARLING had prepared for her meeting with RJ.

She had slightly remade her hair, put on a very conservative powder-blue dress and dark-blue high heels. Her small bag was beige, but was the best she could do at this time.

Her mother's pearl earrings graced her facial features. Faded red lipstick would have to make it, since no other cosmetics were available.

Sandra's late father had given her a German-made silver pin that he had captured during the First World War. It had become an important memory of her father, and she would wear it on special occasions.

She wore it on the upper left side of her dress. Its silver sparkled like new.

RJ wore his newly purchased academy sports jacket, with a white buttoned shirt and tie. The jacket was navy blue, and his tie had blue stripes on it.

He looked like the gentleman that a young lady might be attracted to during this time.

They were dressed quite properly for the meeting that was about to occur.

Dowton's Cafe was indeed busy. It was known for its fish and chips, so to speak. Reservations were actually required. But Sandra did not know of its rule.

Sandra drove her used vehicle into the parking area, adjacent to the entrance.

It was an old Austin sedan, pre-war 1937, without bumpers, and faded paint on most of its body.

The auto had limited mileage on the engine, and it needed two tires that required replacement. (Because of the war, tires and windshield wiper blades were not available.).

However, the radio did work, and the insides were in clean condition.

Most important, Sandra was an excellent driver and she sorely needed the vehicle for transportation to and from her military obligations, etc.

RJ arrived via taxi. They met at the entrance waiting area.

"Wow. Is that you, major?" he greeted her.

"Yes, it is me. I'm sure I must look different to you. I hope it is in a positive way?" she responded.

"Boy, you look sensational. And, to go with your charm you are dynamite. I am overtaken," he returned.

"Compliments will get you everywhere. Thank you. But you are so handsome, you remind me of an American movie star, Mickey Mouse," she humored.

They both laughed. It was to be a great beginning of a long night together.

TWENTY-FIVE

THEY ENJOYED the dinner very much. The fish and chips were excellent.

The atmosphere was outstanding, and the waiter was delightful.

Major Sandra insisted that she go right home as soon as possible for an early rise in the morning to meet upper military officials.

RJ paid the bill, which was not very high due to the economy and military presence in the area.

He walked Sandra to her auto to say goodbye. RJ was to hail a taxi which should be easily accomplished on this main highway.

She asked him to sit in her vehicle for just a few minutes.

He gently opened the passenger side and slipped into the auto.

Sandra thanked him for the lovely dinner and evening, and apologized for having to cut the night short.

"But work obligation comes first and I must rise quite early to be on time. I hope you understand," she stated.

Ending her remarks, she leaned over and planted a meaningful kiss upon his lips.

After she finished embracing him, he came right back and returned his own romantic kiss to her lips that took her by surprise.

He wouldn't let go. Finally, he retreated a bit, keeping his eyes firmly focused on her eyes.

Sandra felt the urge to go further but stopped herself, thinking it would be out of line for now.

When he finally backed off, he held on to her hands and said, "I know that I could now have something special to get this mission safely completed for, not just for the Allies and the free world. You can tell I have really taken to you, in many ways.

"I hope I get to see you again tomorrow, probably in the afternoon. They have scheduled my departure during the following evening.

"Tomorrow they will be picking me up at 0800 hours, taking me directly to army planning headquarters to begin their final operational briefing.

"They said I should use the afternoon to begin to get my things together, which is really giving away most of my personal things. They will keep some smaller items at the academy for me if I am able to return.

"The next day I won't be picked up until 1100 hours, and taken for the final rehearsal. Then, I will be dressed and supplied with the mission items that are to be carried.

"If it is possible, I would love to have you with me during these final hours.

"My final goodbyes will be at sunset.

"I am to board my transportation and depart England."

TWENTY-SIX

COLONEL MALCOMB MCVEY began giving Corporal RJ his formal orders.

"You will be flown to a special airstrip close to the English Channel.

"There you will board a small German aircraft that was captured by our people several weeks ago and will be flown over the channel in the dark and then lit up for a hopeful safe flight across France.

"Your pilot (Captain Peter Peters) is to locate a village named Locust, many miles to the east of Paris.

"When he finds the approximate area, he is to notify you to prepare for your scheduled departure from the craft.

"You are to check and recheck your parachute pack and its release gear, and gather your final items.

"Arriving at the jump doorway, Lieutenant Albert Smithson will be set to firmly open the escape hatch.

"The captain will shout that he has reached the target.

"The doorway is to open. You are to say your goodbyes, hook on to the chute pull bar and jump from the craft.

"Hopefully, you will land on an open area that has large trees at both ends.

"If you have a chance to guide your decent, which may or may not be possible, depending on the wind, and other factors you are to keep away from those trees.

"Landing in the trees could be fatal on impact or at best cause you other physical damage. Also, it would make getting to the ground quite difficult for sure.

"The resistance should be waiting for your drop and will attempt to reach you, as soon as possible.

"If there is enemy in the area, we will not know how that would work out for you. Remember, you have a knife and a small gun attached to your inside right thigh. The gun has six rounds and only six. The knife is retractable.

"Corporal Rankin will have dropped three other chutes of important supplies.

"With luck we are hoping the supplies would land not far from your landing.

"The resistance people will be anxious to gather those supplies.

"If you can help in retrieving the other chutes then please help, as much as possible.

"After accomplishing the mission, or part thereof, we expect you to be transported by them to free France, where underground individuals will be awaiting your safe arrival.

"Our underground will arrange your escape from free France. We are not sure exactly how or when, at this time.

"Key people will introduce themselves to you when possible. They will accept your credentials.

"We have some assurances that you will be treated very well throughout the mission, of course, when possible.

"Our intelligence officers have given us great confidence in your determination and ability to complete this very important mission.

"We will all be waiting for your safe return to our nation and to know that you have completed the mission, to the best of your ability.

"Our prayers will be with you. God bless.

"I must return to general headquarters."

TWENTY-SEVEN

THEY MET the next afternoon. RJ's final training had been completed.

Sandra had somehow taken the day off to spend as much time as possible with him.

She met him in downtown London across from the famous Harrod's department store.

Less than a block away was an area that had been totally bombed out. The smoke was still rising.

RJ stood on the sidewalk in front of Harrod's and took in the view.

He remarked to Sandra, "My country has been training soldiers to come bomb this important city. It is just not acceptable.

"I am more determined than ever to help stop them. Hitler and his murderers must be taken down, and as quickly as is possible. I promise that I will do my part, so help me God."

With tears in her eyes, she reached over and planted a meaningful kiss on the lips of his irritated face, and remarked, "The free world knows you are about to do your very best. We all will be waiting for your safe return and success in your mission.

"Let's get some coffee at the pub across the road. I am very dry and are in need of some liquid. You must be as well."

They waited for the several trucks to move out of their way to walk across to the active pub.

Hand in hand they entered the building and found suitable seats in the far end of the establishment.

They were to spend most of the afternoon at this location.

RJ made a promise to her that if she was to wait for him to return, he would want to share what would be possible together in the future.

She blushed and answered quickly and firmly, "That is the most romantic offer that I have ever received from a man, and I cannot refuse such a wonderful possibility.

"Please, just return safely, and I will be waiting. I don't know what else to say to you at this time. Only God will determine the outcome.

"But isn't it ironic that we should meet under these circumstances and find each other. I have never thought I would find a man while in the service.

"It is a wonderful feeling having an attachment to not only the mission but with you.

"I told my mother about you, and she doesn't believe it. She is, however, very happy for me and of course you, whom she has yet to meet.

"She too will be waiting.

"I am the happiest that I have been for a long time.

"Tomorrow, I will be there when you leave London. I promise you a kiss, hopefully that we will both remember.

"It is now time for me to leave. I know that you have other things to prepare.

"Please get a good night's sleep. You may need it."

Major Sandra said her goodbyes and repeated that special kiss upon his waiting lips.

He escorted her to the Austin sedan.

She immediately started the engine and drove away into the clear sunset.

RJ once again hailed a moving taxi for his return to the academy.

TWENTY-EIGHT

THE DAY OF the beginning of the important mission had arrived.

RJ had experienced a long and quiet sleep.

He knew that this healthy sleep would stand him in good stead.

Lance-Corporal RJ Smidt was ready for action.

He had arrived at the London air base, about two hours early.

The hanger area was crystal clean. Only the small military aircraft was in this storage area.

There was no one appearing in either direction.

It was rather unusually quiet.

All of a sudden, a military jeep drove up in front of the hanger entrance.

Out stepped three uniformed individuals.

One was Captain Oscar Hamm, the very first military officer that he had met when he arrived at his initial meeting location.

Another was a full colonel, Ralph Corson, who was appearing to be the head of this arrival group.

Major Sandra Darling was standing right behind Captain Hamm.

Her effervescing smile immediately caught his eyes.

The colonel began to speak, "I'm glad to finally meet you RJ. I've heard all about you. Fortunately, they were good things, my boy."

He stepped closer and shook his hands.

RJ followed with a salute.

"No need for that right now. We must get you into your mission uniform. Major, you have it all in that large packet.

"Please help him into his attire. Captain, you be sure to check him out," he continued.

"When he is ready, you, Captain Hamm, will fly him to Peacock Strip, as you have been ordered.

"Major, you can go along with them.

"I must leave now, heading back to headquarters.

"I wish you the ultimate luck on your mission. Many people will be counting on your success.

"I pray to God for your personal health during your adventure. My staff will keep me posted. God bless you, son."

The colonel got into the driver's seat of the jeep, started the engine, and drove off into the night.

Captain Hamm and Major Sandra tugged away on his French peasant uniform, as it was to fit him quite tight in all aspects.

Finally, they finished dressing him and distributed the articles that were of major importance in his trip.

Captain Hamm announced, "Let's go, gang. Hop into that little aircraft. She will surely take us to Peacock Strip. It should only take about fifteen minutes to get there. Let's go," he ended.

The three jumped aboard the small airplane. Captain Hamm started the engine. All three were belted into the craft. Out of the hanger and on to the runway they moved.

Within minutes the plane lifted off the tarmac into the evening air headed toward the Peacock Strip, close to the English Channel.

Major Sandra held RJ's hands in the back seats.

TWENTY-NINE

THE SMALL PLANE landed safely on the strip called "Peacock." It was camouflaged from the air and partially protected by trees.

It was difficult to find from the air purposely, to discourage being a bombing target.

Two soldiers came out of the nearby brush to welcome the small craft.

All three disembarked from the cramped vehicle.

They were saluted by the two approaching soldiers.

The soldiers escorted them all to a makeshift office, located behind a bush and leaning against a large walnut tree.

Within the office were two more military ranking officers.

Captain Peter Peters was a pilot, assigned to fly the airplane that would reach the drop target, where RJ was to do his stuff.

The other was Lieutenant Albert Smithson, also a pilot in training, who was to be the co-pilot.

They were ready for RJ.

From under the back trees, they rolled out the captured German Faulkner aircraft.

It had been fueled and checked out, ready for flight.

The plane was designed for three passengers maximum.

It was to carry three and return with only two.

The French peasant was equipped with a special German-type parachute. The other two wore British comparison gear.

They were ready to board the aircraft.

RJ had to say goodbye.

He moved closer to Major Sandra and began planting his parting kiss upon her lips.

She grabbed his whole frame and squeezed. She was not about to let go so quickly.

There were tears in her eyes as she finally let go of him.

It had been a long meaningful embrace as she had promised.

She wiped her tears and stated, "God will bring you home to us. I will pray each day for God's protection and assistance. Please do not try to reach us, under any circumstance. Goodbye for now." She started to cry once again.

Lance-Corporal RJ Smidt turned and saluted for the last time.

He mounted the steps into the captured Nazi aircraft.

The plane sputtered down the narrow strip with its lights off.

When airborne, it headed towards the crossing of the channel, heading for occupied France.

THIRTY

HEADQUARTERS had decided not to tell their defensive forces along the channel about the mission or about the captured airplane that they were about to use to gain access into occupied France.

They felt that at low altitude, during the night, they could avoid detection from their own guns and make it across the channel.

Based on that assumption the return of a Nazi airplane would be almost impossible.

And so, after RJ's drop they were instructed to fly the plane to free France, where they would parachute out and let the plane crash.

The same underground group was to be waiting for their drops somewhere in specified free France.

Then they, too, would be hopefully smuggled out and back to England.

But of course the first step was to get safely to occupied France and to the designated spot for RJ to be dropped.

The mission itself was labeled by headquarters as "Termite."

Operation "Termite" had already begun.

THIRTY-ONE

THE GERMAN PLANE crossed the English Channel without resistance. And it was accomplished without any lights displayed.

Immediately the lights were then operated.

German shore defenses would have spotted the plane and thought it was one of their own surveillance units reporting regularly to Luftwaffe command.

Moving along the occupied French coast and turning inland at low altitude gave them permission to continue toward their vital objective.

The captain, lieutenant, and Corporal RJ talked among themselves.

They couldn't believe how easy it had been to get this far without resistance. Yet, they reminded themselves that they were flying in an enemy plane which appeared normal for the captured sky in that part of France.

The weather had thankfully been pleasant, with cloudy skies and reasonable winds. Rain had been predicted but so far had not arrived.

German aircrafts flew above them in several directions. It was now 0300 hours, darkness still upon them.

The lieutenant, who had taken over the map and directed the movement of the craft announced that the target was getting very near them.

RJ gathered his last-minute things and rechecked his parachute.

"I'm ready when you are. Just come and open the doorway and I'll see you later," he beckoned.

"Okay, corporal. Say your last prayers. I

think I spot the opened field just ahead of us. Yes, it is the basic target area.

"I will circle it twice, to alert your recovery team down below," Captain returned.

The lieutenant yelled, "Look there is a light to the left end of the field. It must be your connection. The light just turned off. That's a good sign."

Lieutenant Smithson left his co-pilot seat and retreated to the doorway.

Captain Peters encircled the target area twice and made his expected command, "This is it. God bless you, son. Open the doorway."

"Thank you for the ride, guys. I'll be seeing you," were RJ's final words as he placed his strap on the hinge point.

Off he jumped into the open night, with his hand on the pull cord that was to open his chute entirely. The chute opened and down he continued.

THIRTY-TWO

AS RJ BEGAN to float downward, he looked back and saw the three other chutes begin to open, carrying valuable supplies, armor, and explosives for the French resistance.

A quick thought went through his mind. The flashing light could have come from the enemy.

He had remembered that Hitler had sent over four million troops to conquer and to hold that portion of occupied France that day.

The German military was supposedly everywhere. *What was really my chance?* he thought.

At that moment he hit what he thought was the ground.

He was wrong. The seat of his pants caught a branch from a tree. Fortunately, it was an outstretched lower branch of an oak tree, at the edge of a thick treed area, at the eastern end of the open field that had been chosen for his drop.

The wind had taken him a bit off course. He had been lucky that he didn't land directly on a tree. It could have been a major physical hit for him and probably would have ruined the mission.

His legs dangled just above the ground. He was able to free himself from the branch and touched the earth beneath him.

Immediately he reached for his stiffly held chute above him and began to pull the strings toward himself.

The chute came together quite well, and he looked for a place to hide it.

Bushes existed to the left, under a smaller oak tree. And so, he deposited the chute behind the tree and into the thickness of the bush.

When he turned around, he was to meet face-to-face with what appeared to be two uniformed Nazi soldiers.

"We are not the enemy. We are the resistance, dressed in captured uniforms, having just returned from a critical killing of fifteen of their search party, who had been threatening an important part of our village.

"There may be retaliation for their losses but we had to do it as it was about to come close to our current headquarters.

"You will learn about this problem later. Are you okay?" he asked in broken English.

"I am Victor LeBlanc, one of our local leaders. My men are chasing the supplies that we have been anxiously awaiting in need.

"Let us get out of this area. It is not usually safe here, but we had to take the chance for your arrival," he finished.

"Our wagon will bring the supplies and all of the chutes.

"We can use this Renault sedan to take us to headquarters," he began once again.

RJ was relieved, to say the least. He had made his drop and contact without fanfare.

What would follow, he did not know.

At this moment he thought of Major Sandra and wished that he could have signaled her to tell of his safe landing and connections after the drop.

The sedan rumbled through the dirt roads to a place in the village.

He did not know the name of this village.

THIRTY-THREE

THE BASEMENT of a small house just three blocks from the downtown village of Boyer, (pronounced boy-a), France had a wooden platform in front of the wash tub.

The platform could be easily moved. It covered an entrance to a tunnel connection to a hidden large room, which became the current headquarters of the local resistance.

The room had been built by a previous owner during the First World War. He had constructed it to protect his family and stored food, wine, and water to survive.

When his young son, who had survived that war took over his family home, he had joined the resistance, and offered them use of its excellent and safe hideaway.

Any movement from the room itself took place only at night. The streets were usually patrolled by the German searchers.

They, of course, were looking for Jews, enemies of the Reich, and any other conspirators that could be brought to their one-sided justice or quickly eliminated.

It was not safe to walk the streets during the daylight. Any and all movement must be carefully attempted at night.

To that end, the resistance had to plan their activities with extreme caution.

Protecting the headquarters was paramount on all activities.

These rules were conveyed to Corporal RJ immediately.

RJ had been introduced to six members of the resistance who were in the room when he arrived there.

All but one was French. The other man was a British Army soldier who had been shot down six months prior and had volunteered to stay with the resistance.

His name was Corporal Roger Palmer, and he was an engineer aboard a fatal aircraft. All eight other members of the plane were killed, either during the crash or by the arriving Nazis.

Corporal Roger Palmer had acted dead and about two hours later was thankfully picked up by the resistance. His legs being crushed, he would doubtfully ever walk again. He was ready to wait out the war with the resistance but could not get involved in RJ's mission.

Roger immediately gravitated to RJ, and they became instant friends.

Homemade muffins and milk were available on a table in the middle of the large room. RJ was to consume more than his share, being very hungry during his trip.

Victor LeBlanc, the leader, had finally returned to headquarters. He and others had located all equipment and supplies that had been dropped to them. The boxes had not yet been opened.

"I'm glad that you have made yourself at home here, and we are now anxious to open your boxes," he stated.

With a small kitchen knife, he began opening the first of several packages on the floor, near the entrance to the hideaway.

The first box opened contained explosives, several different types and sizes. Also included was a written manual to help with installation and detonation.

There was instant talk and discussion. They were all excited about these items, for sure.

The second box had more explosives and a group of hand grenades. Several of the men cheered.

The third box had three automatic machine guns, with some ammunition.

The fourth box was loaded with ammunition. Also in that box was a bag full of maps.

Victor immediately grabbed the maps.

He had a smile on his face.

"These are the tools that we have been waiting for. They will be used to advance our cause quite quickly," Victor stated.

"Thank you, Corporal RJ, for your part in bringing them to us. France will be forever grateful for these items. We will surely make the most from their potential," Victor continued.

"I will study the maps and discuss what important information that Corporal RJ has brought with him."

He dismissed the group for now.

RJ was ready to brief the leader on the latest information that was given to him at yesterday's final briefing.

The second step of his mission was about to begin.

THIRTY-FOUR

CORPORAL RJ SMIDT began submitting important information to the resistance leader, Victor LeBlanc.

"Our double agents have been sending messages to London regularly, since the Nazis invaded France.

"They do it by several different means, and I'm not allowed to know exactly how, but their information is always correct.

"London military headquarters has briefed me on the latest recommendations.

"Much of it is based upon double agents' knowledge and not necessarily from our top officials.

"However, they have located and mapped key positions that, if destroyed, could setback or halt the enemy's movements in Occupied France and elsewhere.

"That's how important this mission could be.

"Because Hitler has sent over four million soldiers and equipment to this area alone, it is believed that their next move would be to include a great portion of the troops and armor from this region.

"Therefore, if you can destroy these key locations, it would greatly stop, or at least temporarily setback, their movement.

"Millions of lives could be saved by such moves, and you are in a position to help make that possible.

"The supplies that have come with me could give you the extra tools to accomplish the objectives.

"I am here to encourage and guide you the best I can and then to escape this area and make my way back to England if possible.

"The maps will support my knowledge of the various plans.

"Let us open the maps and I will attempt to help explain the targets.

"Before we do, I would like to justify to you my reason to be here personally.

"I was born and brought up in Germany.

"When Hitler and his murderers came into power they immediately went after Jews. "Although I am Lutheran, my friends and neighbors were Jews.

"They were taken away and believed to have been terminated. My dad worked for a Jewish company, and they took over the business and killed the ownership.

"Otto, my brother, was recovering from a terrible bout with typhoid fever in a rehabilitation home.

"The Nazis came and took the entire home away. We believe that they were all destroyed.

"My parents wanted to leave Germany, but it had become impossible. Because I had become a history scholar, I was able to enter a contest to visit England as a history representative of the Reich for one year.

"I won the contest and was limited to that one year.

"My parents insisted that I stay in the freedom of England.

"Since then, they have been bombing England and seeking to conquer the world. I cannot let that happen.

"That is why I joined the military, and with my language skills became involved with this mission.

"Now, we can proceed to the maps and plans. I hope you now understand my position here."

THIRTY-FIVE

VICTOR LEBLANC spread the maps out before them.

RJ began pointing to the four major spots that were well circled.

"The first and most important target is in Caen. It is their tank headquarters while in France.

"We are told that about ten officers come and go from this station. A hit to that building would put them into a crisis. Their distribution and implementation would become totally disrupted.

"The building itself is located in this booklet and is printed backwards as a protected code. It was done in case it was captured on me.

"This is a priority target, ordered by our military people.

"The second is located in Rouen. It is a major storage area for fuel and tank supplies. We are told that they send trucks each morning to gain supplies that are needed for each group of Tiger tanks in the greater area. They recommend a night approach only.

"Once again, the directions to find this site are in this booklet, printed backwards.

"The third is situated in Meuse. This is a vital repair and check-out location for tanks only. We have been told that there are at least a dozen tanks there for repair, and must be eliminated.

"And, of course, the actual location is given in the booklet.

"Fourth and final target at this time is located in Marseille, where groups of Tiger tanks are kept, awaiting orders for combat. They believe that there may be as many as one hundred tanks or even more arriving each week. A blow there would be a major setback to their on-going objectives.

"The booklet offers several considerations that could be used in your plans.

"Obviously, this booklet is now in your hands. It had been sown into the lining of my outer jacket.

"Do you have any questions? I hope that I can be of help in any way that would lead to completing this mission.

"That's why I was chosen."

Victor replied, "No, not at this time. Your people have put together excellent details for us to basically follow.

"We are already in great debt for this information and your support.

"Tomorrow we will begin to address these targets. My people will be getting involved in the actual plans at that time.

"Enough for now, let us get some sleep. We will need everything going for us tomorrow evening."

There was a mattress put in the corner of the large room for RJ.

Within minutes he began sleeping.

The next day was but a few hours away.

THIRTY-SIX

FIRST THING in the morning the leader, Victor LeBlanc, called a meeting of his fellow volunteers.

Coffee, tea, and toast were offered to all.

Seven men and two women arrived.

They were dressed in peasant decorum and immediately sat down on the several benches that had been setup for the meeting.

Victor began, "We have received important information and supplies to approach four major targets, of which our visitor has come here to thankfully assist.

"They have asked us to go to Caen for the first important target.

"It is a building that contains much of the control team that regularly orders movement of their prize Tiger tanks.

"We are to destroy the building. It must be done at night.

"We'll need four individuals to help Corporal RJ Smidt and myself in the operation.

"I asked Miriam to be one of them. Leon would be the logical detonator that must be along.

"The other two can be any of you. Please raise your hands if you are desirous to accompany this challenge."

Midge Colin, Peter Weas, and Adrian LeForge quickly raised their hands.

Victor quickly added, "Only two more can come. Midge and Peter raised first.

"The remaining five of you should work on supplies and inspection on our weapons that we will be taking with us.

"Midge, Miriam, Leon, and Peter stay right here and we will begin to go over the particulars for tomorrow's work."

Now there were six committed for tomorrow's effort. They included Victor and RJ, along with the other four.

The six gathered around the map table and Victor went about explaining the plans.

RJ made sure he covered all the information that was available.

Victor promised that he would go over the plans once again tomorrow morning or early afternoon.

It appeared that they were basically set for the first target to be attempted tomorrow evening in Caen.

THIRTY-SEVEN

RESISTANCE volunteers Stella Bours and husband Andre were farmers, delivering mostly hay to the occupied Nazis for their horses located in several barnyards that they had taken over in occupied France.

Andre drove an old flat-bed truck, which had been secretly used by the resistance in many of their planned work.

He regularly made deliveries to their stables and coming and going was more-often waved through inspection areas without stopping.

Victor spoke to Andre for permission to use his wagon once again for the transportation of the individuals and equipment for target number one.

Built under his wagon was a large leather hammock to secure safely two individuals for a limited time.

It had been successfully used in several prior planned programs.

Victor predicted that it would take two trips to Caen in order to get everyone and the equipment to the staged area.

Andre was to locate the waiting place and, of course, the layout of the target itself.

He had already left to hopefully get that important information.

Upon his return, Victor would be given his information, needed for an early meeting with the whole group the next morning.

When morning arrived, Victor had in his hands a lay-out and expected waiting place, before beginning the actual work.

Victor began his assignment.

"Miriam will ride with Andre on the first run. Packed in the very last bale of hay will be machine guns and ammunition.

"Under the truck will be Leon and Peter. The second run will have Midge with Andre in the truck, and Peter and I underneath.

"Corporal RJ will not go on this mission. He'll be waiting for our return. We hope it will be a safe one.

"All of us will return, with one of us with Andre, in the truck itself, two others underneath and the rest hidden under the canvas spread over the flat-bed, hiding under it.

"It will be our only source of escape.

"Andre will be ready for us when we are finished with the set-up at the facility.

"Hopefully, all the plans should go right.

"Andre will be ready to leave for the first run in about an hour. Please get ready to

THIRTY-EIGHT

ANDRE brought them to a destroyed farm in the outskirts of Caen.

It had been bombed previously and completely abandoned by the Nazis.

It allowed them to hide, await darkness and the timing for their plot.

There was enough water and food brought in to last a whole day, if necessary. The chances of being discovered there were few.

Yet, there were Nazi patrols in the area regularly.

Andre had taken his wagon into town to get some dinner. His empty wagon was visible to all while it was parked.

He had delivered all of the hay that had brought him to the area.

Andre knew that he needed to bring all of the individuals and the supplies close to the target about thirty minutes prior to detonation.

He had about an hour to waste downtown.

The restaurant was full of Nazi soldiers and some officers. They left him alone at a table near the door.

Finally, it was time for him to go get Victor and his group and to bring them very close to the target. His instructions called for him to remain nearby and to be prepared to make a quick get away without drawing attention to his vehicle.

Darkness had appeared and the target had been closed and locked.

They must have left a security guard inside the building.

Andre had reached the farm in the outskirts and had loaded the group aboard. The supplies were hidden under the canvas, closest to the cab of the truck.

Miriam, holding a machine gun, was riding in front with Andre. Midge and Peter were under the canvas, while Victor and Leon were under the truck in the leather hammock.

They approached the target via the back street. There were no lights in the rear of the building.

Immediately, the canvas was put aside and the supplies were given out.

Midge and Miriam were holding machine guns for cover.

Leon, Peter, and Victor each grabbed boxes of dynamite and moved slowly and quietly to the frame of the facility.

All three sides were to be gifted explosives. The front was deliberately left alone, as front was displayed from the main street.

Within fifteen minutes the dynamite was installed along the framework of this important building.

Leon was to set all of them for detonation, estimated for about twenty minutes, no more.

He was the last to get back into the truck.

Victor and one side of the leather hammock were waiting for his arrival, the engine had been started. Andre and Miriam were waiting for his tap from underneath that he had returned to his hammock hide-away. The tap was heard by all of them. Andre put the truck into gear and off they went toward home.

Sure enough, about twenty minutes into the return they heard the distant explosions that rocked the area.

They were far away from any suspicious inspection of that section.

The target had appeared to have been eliminated as planned.

Their return was uneventful.

The number one target had been successfully completed without using a bullet.

Corporal RJ and others were elated to hear the news.

TheNazis control center for their tanks had been destroyed and it was to set back plans for their special use and deployments.

Victor broke out some vintage wine and they all celebrated.

THIRTY-NINE

AFTER celebrating their success of target number one, Victor began talking about target number two.

It would be for tomorrow.

That target involved destroying fuel locations and supplies in Rouen.

Victor stated that Andre's hay wagon would have to be used for this one as well.

Corporal RJ would be included in this goal, and he was ready to go.

Victor called for a meeting early the next morning to fill in the details of his plan.

Nazi patrols would surely be active around this crucial location.

Getting to this area would be more difficult, to say the least.

Victor talked about his concern to penetrate the Nazi protection. He warned everyone that hand-to-hand fighting would be necessary to get through to the actual target.

Tomorrow would be an important and dangerous day for sure.

He asked everyone to get rest and to be prepared for tomorrow's encounter. Victor stated, "Some of us may not return from this objective."

Just then, the hideaway door opened and in walked Andre's wife, Stella, carrying a tray of freshly baked French pastries.

It was to enliven the celebration once again.

More wine appeared and some French songs were sung softly between three of them.

"It's okay," Victor responded.

"Let us enjoy the rest of this day," he continued.

Tomorrow would soon be upon them.

FORTY

HIS MEETING was called to order at 0700.

Victor began, "If our plan is to succeed, we might have to fight our way through Nazi defenses, which should be stationed around the target area.

"They will be sitting in small vehicles and trucks.

"There should not be any tanks or armored equipment at the entrance stations.

"The actual complex has a wired fence around the entire area. There is only one guard walking around the perimeter of the fence at all times.

"Most of the fuel is in the storage areas, almost touching the wire fence.

"The darkness should allow us to see the guard, and to be able to study his route around the outside fence.

"We need to get to the fence in the rear section to be able to throw our grenades and explosives directly into those storage areas and escape.

"There is only one entrance way, and it will be easily observed by us.

"If the guard, or anyone else, should see us and our action, they will surely attempt to go after us.

"It looks like the only way they could come after us, would be through that single entrance. So, that is in our favor.

"We will not have coverage so it will be our own ability to escape.

"Andre and his truck will be waiting around the very first corner, completely out-of-sight from the fuel facility. His engine will be going, awaiting our quick return.

"Then, we will be expecting to past the probable road-block area that they would want to impose.

"They could become satisfied with a house-to-house search and street-to-street as well. If things go well, we could be well beyond their searching area.

"As you can see, a speedy jump from the target is crucial.

"Our escape could become difficult, and our weapons and surprise will be hopefully enough to get us out of the proximity of the target location.

"Those that are not part of this program will be expected to get the proper supplies together. Also, don't forget some food and drink for us.

"We will be leaving soon, in the daylight, to arrive before darkness to prepare for the actual movement.

"The timing of our assault will be important, but weather conditions could change our approach timing.

"Only time will tell."

FORTY-ONE

THEY BEGAN their trip to Rouen. Andre was driving his wagon-truck.

Leon was traveling in front with Andre. He held tightly because under his seat was an automatic machine gun, to be used if necessary.

Corporal RJ and Victor were under the bed of the vehicle in the leather pouch with smaller automatic weapons.

The body of the truck carried hay, except in the rear cradled against the cab was the explosive supplies. A bag of food and drinks were kept on the front seat floor.

They worked their way toward Rouen without having to stop.

When arriving in Rouen, Andre knew exactly where to drop off some hay and then head directly to the spot he was to wait.

It was around the first corner from the fuel depot location.

They would now have to wait about an hour for darkness to arrive.

The food and drink bag was opened and distributed.

Soon darkness had arrived.

Victor left the hide-away and walked to the corner.

There, he could observe the current situation of the building and grounds.

He noted that everything appeared to be as expected.

Victor could see the guard walking around the wired fence. The guard carried a rifle over his right shoulder. His movement was quite slow.

Victor timed the guard's revolution around the fence. It was clearly twelve minutes for him to return to the planned point of detonation.

He now had enough information to share with Leon and Corporal RJ.

"It appears very much as planned. We will have about ten minutes to do the job and begin our return to the truck.

"If everything goes right, we should be able to complete our throws and begin our run within the ten minutes.

"Hopefully, we won't be detected before our run and won't need to fire our weapons. But we won't know beforehand if that will work out.

"Someone in the interior of the fence may spot us at any phase of the operation. There could be immediate gun fire. "That's why we carry guns and often-times have to fire them.

"Once again, our quick return to the truck is imperative.

"The three of us should get our grenades and then LET'S GO.

"May God bless us and France," he finished.

The three men turned the corner, and slowly walked towards the target.

FORTY-TWO

THEY REACHED a point about two-hundred yards from the rear of the fence, close to the exact target position for them to launch their explosives.

Victor motioned to get down and crawl the two-hundred yards to the target position.

The outside fence guard had just turned the corner and disappeared behind the building. He would be coming around the building to within view of them in about nine minutes.

Victor whispered, "Let's stand up and get the job done," and he rose from the ground.

Leon and RJ followed him.

The three began whirling their hand grenades, five each.

When they completed, they turned and ran.

The explosions rocked the place, and all around them.

Victor, Leon, and RJ ran as fast as they could into the darkness.

When they reached the corner, the fuel depot was in total flames and several smaller explosions continued.

The area was lit with daylight from the fire and flames. Additional lighting came from the vehicles within the compound starting their engines.

It appeared that they had been caught in surprise.

The main gate was quickly opened and the first military vehicle began to leave the compound.

Other vehicles followed and they began their pursuit to find the culprits.

Sirens began to blast away and the community rose quickly to see what had happened.

The three runners reached the truck and jumped quickly into their get-away positions.

Andre had the engine revving and quickly put it in gear.

They rumbled their way into the main get-away route and began mixing with other trucks that were, or had been, delivering goods to the local area.

Andre followed the returning route, making their way towards the outer limits of the Nazis' expected roadblocks.

It sure looked like they had made their get-away safely when an unexpected roadblock appeared before them.

There were four vehicles ahead of them, three trucks and one bus.

The bus had been guided out of line and moved to the front, and was waiting to be inspected. There was an armored vehicle aside of the actual roadblock, with several armed soldiers. Three other soldiers were conducting the inspections.

Andre was not concerned, but Leon in the front seat cab with him was concerned. He had to hide the automatic weapon that was under his seat.

He then put his jacket over the rifle to help minimize the view. His fingers were crossed as the vehicle moved forward.

Andre spoke loudly to the whole group. "I am confident that we will pass this inspection very quickly. I know how to handle these soldiers. Just keep quiet and I'll handle it all."

This Nazi inspection team was very thorough. They were well trained to look for conspirators and wanted individuals.

Fortunately, they became ready to inspect the bus at the time that Andre had brought the truck to the front of the inspection line.

And so, the inspection team went to work inspecting the bus, the exterior, their credentials, and the interior's group of workers, who were being returned to their camp not far from this point.

The lead inspection officer's phone began ringing and he finally answered it.

It appeared that he was being told of the depot explosion and the possible look-out for the fleeing culprits.

They reported that the explosions had been detonated about forty-five minutes ago and that they surely hadn't reached their outpost at this time.

With that information, the officer decided to let the next three vehicles go through without inspection and he asked for several of the soldiers, who had been waiting aside the roadblock in the military vehicle, to come closer to the inspection location.

Andre had been correct. They were not to be inspected. He did not have to address his existence as he had been prepared to do.

The hay truck rambled on toward their headquarters.

It had been a successful event without bloodshed.

The second target had been hit as planned, and much fuel had been destroyed as the mission had requested.

FORTY-THREE

WHEN THEY arrived home, there was great celebration.

More wine and homemade food awaited their heroes.

Victor once again, with a smile, began to talk about target number three.

"Please, don't let this spoil the celebration. We all deserve it.

"But tomorrow we must attempt target number three.

"This next objective is to help destroy a tank repair location in Meuse.

"We have been told that there would be some dozen or more tanks, mostly Tiger type, being reconstructed or having been completed awaiting pick-up by their trained tank leaders.

"A good hit there could slow their movement not only in France, but in surrounding countries on their current list for aggression.

"We need to do our best here with surprise as well.

"The Nazi command may think that this could also be one of our targets and could have built up security there.

"We won't know for sure until we get there. But we must be ready for the worst that could happen.

"Our meeting will begin at 0700 hours tomorrow. Please don't be late," he finished.

Andre Bours's wife, Stella, went around kissing and hugging all of the resistance men. Even Lance-Corporal RJ Smidt got his on both cheeks.

Victor did his best to finish a half-full bottle of wine that had been put before him.

Soft humming and singing continued for the next hour.

RJ wanted to get some sleep as soon as possible. He sought clear thinking for the next day's objective.

Finally, the celebration came to a close.

RJ excused himself and dropped onto his mattress-bed in the far corner of the large room.

Once again, tomorrow had presented concerns for all of them.

But the new day was just a few hours away.

FORTY-FOUR

EVERYONE WAS present at 0700 hours.

Victor started explaining the assignment. "Andre's truck must be used once again.

"I will be in the cab with Andre. A weapon will be under my seat, as was with the others who had sat there as well.

"The two leather pockets under the wagon will have Leon and Corporal RJ.

"Behind the hay load, close to the cab of the truck, will be both Peter and Miriam with automatic rifles.

"Each of us will carry four hand grenades. Other explosives will be put into the last bale of hay.

"We will leave early, about 1000 hours, less than three hours from now.

"Our target is located on the rural approach to the city of Meuse.

"We cannot get too close to our objective. They have positioned the tanks in wide open space.

"There should be guards as well, creating cover and security to the entrance area.

"A daily password may be in use, and getting through into the yard might be quite difficult.

"But we may have to fight our way through the gate entrance, just to get to the main group of tanks.

"The main group is our most important target. If we can get there, the damage to these tanks could alter the movement of the war.

"We cannot chance losing Corporal RJ, so he will be left behind in the truck.

"Andre will take up arms and protect our rear, leaving Corporal RJ in the driver's seat. RJ will keep the truck's engine going and prepare for a quick get-away.

"The rest of us will be ready to advance through that entrance to make it to the main group of tanks.

"Each of us will be carrying explosives that need to be thrown against the tracks of the tanks. Our hand grenades can do the same damage.

"The tracks on their Tigers are our easy prey. They cannot move on broken tracks.

"Repair or replacement of tracks can take weeks, maybe even months to complete. It is our best bet to stop the advancement of these critical and superior tanks.

"If we are lucky, we could come out of there without much actual combat, but we won't know that until we get there.

"We will have to destroy the guards at least to enter the compound.

"At night, there shouldn't be repair people at the location. The entrance guards could be their only defenses.

"Those who are not going with us should be preparing other needs for us now.

"The list includes putting fuel into the truck, loading of hay and checking our weapons and loading the ammunition and explosives.

"Also, please prepare food, water, and some first aid supplies.

"Are there any questions?" he finished.

The time to leave for this mission was only an hour and minutes away.

FORTY-FIVE

THEY DELIVERED two bales of hay to a farm, where several Nazi soldiers were scolding the farmer, his young son, and wife, while Andre and Victor slowly took the bales off the rear of his truck.

One soldier walked his way over to the truck and began yelling at them in German.

Smartly, Andre and Victor continued going about their business of unloading, and the soldier turned away and began walking back to join the other soldiers.

Andre drove off as quickly as possible without calling any further attention to his vehicle.

Just before darkness he made a run by the target compound.

They sighted the entrance, noting two guards there, one in the guard house and the other standing at the gate itself.

No other military defenses were observed. It looked like an easy task before them.

The distance between the covered area where their truck would be waiting and the compound's entrance was approximately four blocks, much further distance than their previous missions.

Victor explained, "We will be running quite a distance, returning from our destination. And, remember, we cannot leave any of our equipment or supplies behind.

"Make sure your shoes are tied well.

"Darkness is almost upon us.

"I am now ready to pray to God for our safe return.

"Please take a minute to thank God."

The packed food was distributed and they quietly consumed what had been given to them.

Darkness had now arrived.

They slowly gathered their equipment and came together outside the truck.

They were each loaded with arms, explosives, and hand grenades, and ready to go to mission number three.

FORTY-SIX

THE WIND had increased but the weather was warm and there was no sign of rain.

Victor led his Resistance group slowly across the open area.

He had with him Leon, Peter, and Miriam, each fully equipped with automatic weapons and explosives.

Corporal RJ was left in the driver's seat at the vehicle as planned.

Being hidden by the darkness of the evening, they approached the entrance to the compound.

The outside guard began shouting, "Who goes here?" in German.

Victor's rifle had a silencer and he quickly hit the guard twice. The guard dropped to the ground.

Out of the guard house came the second guard with rifle in hand.

Miriam shot him twice. He fell quickly, about a foot away from the other guard.

The noise from her shots could be heard at great distance.

It must have alerted other military people, causing immediate action to be organized.

Victor and his group ran into the compound and kept running to the target area before them.

Grenades and explosives began exploding in several directions.

They had been hitting target after target, damaging the under-tracks of possibly fifty Tiger tanks.

It was time for their get-away.

They had emptied their grenades and explosives and had begun running back through the entrance gate into the open area.

All of a sudden, rifle fire came at them.

Leon took a hit. His right shoulder had been injured.

Victor fell down and bruised his left knee. He quickly arose and continued running.

Miriam started firing back, not knowing exactly where the enemy was located.

She took a hit on the handle of her automatic weapon, but luckily escaped further firing and kept on running.

They had finally reached the limit of the soldiers' rifle firing. But they had much further to go to the waiting truck.

As they looked back, they saw lights from all directions, indicating the probable assembly of a military response, sure to be converging in the area.

They knew that their quick get-away was imperative.

As planned, Corporal RJ had the engine warming and when they all arrived, quickly took up their original positions in the truck.

Andre jumped back into the driver's seat, with Corporal RJ moving over to the other position.

It appeared that they had completed their mission, and now to get away.

Andre was aware of the streets leading to the main road out of the city of Meuse.

Once beyond the city limits, they would feel reasonably safe, as one would think even a quick get-away would not have passed through the city.

There was no sign of road blocks.

It appeared that their escape had been successful.

They drove quite slowly along the exterior roads towards the headquarters.

Everyone was exhausted. Leon had his shoulder taped and bandaged, Miriam's weapon would have to be repaired, and Victor's knee would have to be examined when they arrived back at their hide-away.

It was only a token price to pay for a great mission accomplished.

Some fifty Tiger tanks were now put out-of-order for at least a long period of the on-going war.

One would have to believe that many lives may have been saved by the success of this important mission.

These individuals will certainly sleep well tonight.

FORTY-SEVEN

A DAY OF rest was in order and Victor announced it to everyone.

He expected to sleep a good part of the day and then work on their final mission that Corporal RJ had brought with him.

They decided not to celebrate target number three, which they had just completed.

Instead Leon recommended holding up any party until completing the next and final important mission. No one seemed to object.

Corporal RJ was openly pleased with the results so far. He was however anxious to finish the list and attempt to make it back to England.

He constantly reminded himself of Major Sandra Darling waiting for his return, and his hopes of including her in his future.

Victor LeBlanc had arisen from his sleep and wanted to begin planning for the final phase.

Corporal RJ and Victor, along with Leon, gathered on the floor of the large room.

Spread between them were maps and the booklet, which held recommendations.

This target was in Marseille and would require every available individual.

The list included Victor, Leon, Peter, Andre, Miriam, Midge, Adrian, Pierre, Andre's wife, Stella, and Corporal RJ.

Victor began, "I have decided that several of them must travel to Marseille by train or bus.

"Train would be safer and quicker but bus might be easier to pass interrogations.

"Andre and his truck must once again be used effectively.

"Driving the vehicle would be Andre, and Stella would ride in the second seat.

"In the leather pouches below the truck will be Corporal RJ and me.

"It leaves Leon, Peter, Miriam, Midge, Adrian, and Pierre to arrive by bus or train.

"They all have identifications for work in the fields and elsewhere.

"It would be cheaper and less visual by bus.

"We must be sure that connections would bring them to Marseille on time, before darkness. Midge is already checking bus schedules, etc.

"If this mission is to work, we must be ready and prepared for every detail.

"Fortunately, Andre knows the area quite well. He has been delivering hay to the farms and supply locations in the Marseille limits for many years and they know him there, which could be helpful.

"His vehicle must be loaded with fuel, hay, and extra covers.

"He will be delivering all the hay on the way before darkness.

"We must meet up with the others just before the sunset.

"Andre will tell us exactly where.

"From the bus or train station, a taxi should be able to take them to Andre's place for meeting, located hopefully close to our target.

"We will have under the covers on the truck weapons, ammunitions, and hand grenades for each of us to do the job.

"When we complete our assignment, we will escape totally on and in the truck.

"This could be the most dangerous mission thus far, and all of us may not be coming back.

"All identification should be left in the truck before the attempt.

"Obviously, if any of us are caught, we must protect the location of our important home base."

FORTY-EIGHT

THEY AWOKE to an exceptional day of weather.

The sky was clear, showing a medium blue with few clouds, and it was warm.

Victor LeBlanc had already completed his basic plans. He was waiting for transportation reports.

Midge entered the large room.

"Only one train per week is allowed right now. They are being used for troop transport to key spots along the various borders.

"It appears that Hitler is getting ready for further advancements.

"The bus is available. It can take approximately four hours via two transfers to get to Marseille. French francs are still acceptable on the buses.

"A first bus would leave our town in two hours and arrive with plenty of time to spare. I would suggest taking the first bus, allowing extra time, just in case of problems that we are not aware of," Midge ended.

Victor replied, "Yes, the bus should be used and the first one would be important to take.

"Please prepare to go by foot to the bus station in less than two hours."

And so, the group of six, Leon, Peter, Miriam, Midge, Adrian, and Pierre, began helping each other ready for the mission.

Victor would check them, going over the plan, etc. before they would begin their walk toward the bus terminal several blocks away.

Andre's truck was being loaded with the vital weapons and supplies, plus the bales of hay, to be delivered along the way.

Corporal RJ wanted to go over the plan once again. Victor gladly sat down with him, Andre, and Stella.

Victor cautioned again, "We don't know what to expect of their security. The grounds are sure to be heavily guarded.

"I think we will have to fight our way in and out to accomplish our mission."

Soon, the plan began.

FORTY-NINE

THE GROUP of six had boarded the bus.

They had been interrogated prior to boarding. Nothing unusual had been detected by their common movement or identifications.

Andre's truck began its journey, packed with the tools of the mission.

The countryside was still full of farms, although many had been overtaken by the Nazi soldiers.

Still, Andre knew where to make his deliveries, and several were just ahead of them.

Stella would help Andre drag the bales off the rear of the truck.

She was strong and knew almost as much as her husband Andre. He would tell his peers that she could drive and deliver without him, if necessary.

Two roadblocks had been passed.

Andre's truck had been waved through. He had been a regular vendor that the Nazis believed important.

Fortunately, this advantage was critical to their missions, as it was today.

It was mid-afternoon when they completed the deliveries of hay.

They were now in the outskirts of Marseille.

Andre drove his truck to a tavern, just a walking block from one of the several entrances to the tank parking lot, the target.

He put the truck in the back of the tavern, where there was an old shack used for storage by the tavern owner.

Haim Bentberger owned the tavern.

He was an Austrian Jew and he had been forcefully taken away by the Nazis to a concentration camp in Poland.

They replaced him by hiring Norman Whisler, whom had become a resistance fighter, unknown to the Nazis.

Norman had made an important friendship with Andre and his wife.

Andre had made use of his old shack twice before and now he had told Norman that this use would be vital to the success of an attempt to slow-down the Nazi's Tiger tanks advancements.

Norman volunteered to do anything to help the cause.

He promised to have cold drinks and sandwiches awaiting them all in the shack.

They had arrived quite early, and would be awaiting the arrival of the six, scheduled to arrive via taxis from the nearby bus station.

Andre and Victor decided to visit the pub.

They walked around the building and came through the main entrance.

The pub was full of Nazi soldiers imbibing and eating.

It was probable that many were preparing to take control of Tiger tanks that were, but a block away.

Andre and Victor took seats and ordered beers. Norman personally delivered the drinks. He would not take their money.

Norman spoke quietly to Victor. "Their vehicles are left open to the sides of our building. You may want to set something upon them to bring the attention away from your mission."

Victor replied, "You are very special Norman. We won't forget you when this war is over.

"Thank you for your genius advice. We may take up your recommendation."

Norman returned to the bar and the noise.

Andre and Victor finished their beers and left the tavern, returning to the shack, where Corporal RJ and Stella were sitting on two bales of hay, and drinking wine, which had been supplied by Norman as well.

They decided to attach an explosive to a military vehicle nearest the shack when darkness arrived.

The potential diversion would become a great advantage in their attempt to fulfill the mission.

When would the six other individuals arrive? It was getting late.

Darkness was nearly there, and still no taxis.

All of a sudden, two taxis came through the back street and stopped just short of the shack.

Out came the group of six individuals, led by Leon.

He exclaimed to Victor, "We were afraid to arrive too early here and waited until almost dark to take the trip. There were several enemy vehicles in the area of the bus station and we didn't want to cause any attention to our group."

Victor returned, "Nice going, but we were worried that we would have to do the job without you guys."

They all entered the shack and participated in the collation that pub owner Norman had planned for them. The sandwiches were of ham, pork, and chicken, all on dark German rye bread, with small amounts of mustard on each sandwich.

Beer, water, and terrible coffee were there for drinking.

Darkness came within twenty minutes of the group of six's arrival.

Victor was ready to give his last instructions.

He began, "There is one of several gates just across the next block.

"Another gate is about two blocks to the right.

"Each gate has one guard, armed and stationed there, not to move.

"There appears to be a vehicle which roams the entire circumference of the large grouping of Tigers.

"We have been told he makes it around approximately in thirty-minute segments, even if he should take time to urinate or eat.

"It is imperative that we time his rounds to get our advantage. We guess that there are probably four more gates surrounding the complex, but we are only interested in these two for our mission.

"We will all get equipped with weapons and hand grenades. I have the only weapon with a silencer.

"Together we will approach the first gate in the darkness.

"When the moving vehicle passes or begins his rounds, passing gate one closest to us, I will encourage the guard to come out of his booth and shoot him, clearing the gate for us.

"We should storm the opening and begin running four to the left and four to the right.

"Miriam is to run to the second gate and take out that guard and open that gate in case we need it.

"Timed approximately three minutes of a run, stop, and begin firing at the tracks of their Tigers, grenades when two are close to each other.

"Your weapons alone can create damage to the tracks, so don't forget to use up much of your ammunition on any and all tanks within your area.

"Within ten minutes everyone should have done plenty of damage to their tanks and we would need to run back to the shack and the truck.

"In escaping, Andre and Stella will be in the cab and Corporal RJ and I will be tucked away under the truck.

"The rest of you must get into the rear of the truck and hide beneath the canvas or covers provided.

"Andre knows his way out of here, and we all will be trusting him to get us back as safe as possible.

"Are there any questions? We don't know what kind of a response from them will occur, but do what you have to do to get back to the shack.

"God Bless us all."

FIFTY

LEON FOUND the vehicle closest to the shack side of the building. It was a military adapted Volkswagen.

An explosive was set underneath the engine compartment.

He set it with a rather short fuse, which would surely get the vehicle away from the tavern and probably close to an entrance gate on the other side of the compound.

Victor led the group across the street in the darkness and approached the first gate area.

He signaled for the group to wait and began moving towards the gate.

Victor threw a rock toward the gatehouse.

As expected, the guard came running out.

Victor fired at him with his silencer. The guard fell face first to the pavement.

Victor quickly signaled the group to run through the gate and go in either of the two directions.

They quickly went running in both of those directions.

And yes, about three minutes of their running, stopped, and began firing at the tracks of each Tiger tank in their areas.

Victor had gone up the middle and began firing at the same time.

The explosion of the military vehicle was heard in the distance.

Victor turned to see the lights and the smoke coming from the explosion. Leon had done a great job.

It was believed that most of the military attention went towards the explosion, but the guards from the other guardhouses began shooting towards The Resistance members who were destroying the tracks of their prize tanks.

Peter got hit in his back and fell to the ground. He continued throwing his grenades and fired his weapon repeatedly.

Pierre saw him go down and worked his way over to help him gain his strength to stand and run with him.

He ran as fast as he could, which was not very fast at all. Other shots were being sent towards them as they ran.

Miriam had killed the guard at gate two, as requested.

She emptied her rounds and grenades as she began running towards gate one.

Andre took a hit across the chest. He hobbled down gate one, hoping to get back to the truck first and to get it started. The pain in his chest caused him to slow up when he reached the gate itself.

Thankfully, Midge had finished her damage portion and had set up at the gate to protect a response.

Three soldiers came over the horizon and began firing.

Midge used her automatic weapon and killed all three of them.

More German soldiers were coming over that horizon running toward the gate as Victor, Pierre, and Peter were right behind Miriam and Andre in retreat.

The German soldiers began firing. Midge received a hit in the head and began ducking behind the gate itself.

They caught her right arm and then her chest. She fell.

Midge was left to die. No one could go back for her anyway.

Corporal RJ, Adrian, and Leon all came through the second gate.

Miriam's removal of the second gate guard had made that possible.

All but Midge had made it somehow beyond the gates and into the darkness, moving at a pace towards the shack when the German roving vehicle, which had made a complete circle around the compound, returned to gate one.

Victor instructed everyone to quickly board the truck and to begin their escape.

Stella had to inform Victor that Andre had been hit in the chest and that she would be doing the driving.

The cost of the mission had included the death of Midge, the chest wound to Andre, and a bullet into Peter's back.

Victor would memorialize Midge to her family, a brother and two sisters, upon returning.

Stella patched up Andre the best she could. He sat in pain in the front seat next to her.

They had successfully completed the mission, having destroyed possibly hundreds of tracks to the main volume of advanced Tiger tanks waiting to be put into use for future aggression by the Nazis.

Damage to their tracks could easily derail those superior tanks for months or even years.

Later, they were told that the Allies had bombed their only known track manufacturing plant in Frankfort.

Corporal RJ Smidt had completed his targeted assignment and was now thinking about leaving The Resistance and attempting to get back to England.

The ride back to their headquarters was slow, without having to stop at the two roadblocks thankfully.

Guards at both roadblocks quickly observed that the hay had been delivered and that the back was empty, but with canvas, etc. and waved it through.

The day had ended and they were thankful

for the success. The celebration was dimmed by the loss of Midge and the wounds to Andre and Peter.

But they partied anyway, imbibing wine, cake, and pastries.

Victor excused himself and went to visit Midge's relatives.

Later, he returned and attempted to celebrate with the rest.

Tomorrow, they would begin making connections with the Free France underground and to find the way to get Corporal RJ Smidt out of Occupied France.

FIFTY-ONE

ANDRE HAD the bullet taken out of his chest and was feeling better the next morning. Stella had given him some powerful medication.

Victor asked Andre to meet up with Conrad LaPort, Resistance member, who had been working with the Nazis, giving them information about agricultural locations where they might obtain food for their soldiers.

Conrad had connections with known underground individuals who were bringing in unapproved items that included wine and whiskey from Scotland and other connections.

Many of his clandestine items came from Free France, including Casablanca in Morocco.

Victor thought that maybe Conrad could include Corporal RJ in one of his trips to Free France.

If this could be done, they would immediately contact the underground there to find a legitimate transit to get him out of this part of Europe and hopefully back to England.

Andre, who knew Conrad better than others in the group, volunteered to approach Conrad that day.

Conrad wanted to cooperate on the plan. He quickly called in his markers to get the effort in motion.

Corporal RJ Smidt was ready to go. His generic French peasant uniform was by now well-worn and more typical of the average local Frenchman on the streets.

His identification card was still in order, and his French language had gotten better during his stay.

RJ had said his goodbyes to everyone before leaving.

He thanked them for their cooperation and for his safe protection.

"I wish you the best of luck in your fight to once again free your country," he ended.

Andre was ordered to take Corporal RJ to a meeting point on the other side of town.

It was an abandon market that had been closed down by the Nazis.

The back door was opened, and a man stood there apparently waiting.

Corporal RJ was told to enter the market.

The man at the door turned out to be a captain in the French Legion, who himself was in hiding from the Nazis.

He began, "There is a German airplane due to land on that schoolyard tonight.

"It will have two or three soldiers who will accept you aboard to fly with them to a Casablanca airfield.

"There, they will be loading whiskey and beer that will be delivered back to some Nazi officials, without the headquarters knowing.

"This was Conrad's way of keeping close to important officers and their information.

"The aircraft had engine trouble. It stalled out twice, but somehow it made a decent landing at the right airfield."

Obviously, Corporal RJ was to leave that airfield at once.

He had been told that a vehicle would be there to meet him when landed.

A woman driver awaited the Corporal.

She was an armed attractive brunette, with a big welcoming smile.

"I am Adele. You must be RJ, yes?" she spoke.

"Yes, I am RJ. Glad to meet you," he responded.

RJ was pleased to see a pretty woman once again.

She drove for several miles to reach a run-down fishing village.

There, she parked the vehicle next to a fishing wharf.

Adele stated, "You are to go into that small house ahead of us, introduce yourself to Oscar and Van. Then, find some food and drink and relax. You will be escorted tomorrow to the city's large airport.

"I am told that you will be going to Barcelona, Spain, if everything goes well. Good luck to you. I must leave now."

Corporal RJ met his hosts and found food and drink.

Soon, he would be fast asleep, dreaming about freedom, England, and Major Sandra Darling.

FIFTY-TWO

CORPORAL RJ was picked up at 0900 hours by Adele once again and brought to the large airport.

Adele spoke, "You are a nice-looking man. I hope to find one like you after this terrible war is finished. I wish you a good flight."

He responded, "Thank you, and for the driving that you have completed. I must go."

The airport was full of Nazi soldiers and equipment in every direction. He felt like he was back in Germany.

Interrogators were everywhere, checking on flight plans and transits.

His transit stated, "To locate precious metals for a French factory that had been taken over by the Nazis." He was to return on the last plane leaving Barcelona. The transit was approved by local headquarters and signed by two German officers.

The first interrogator let him go without reading the authority portion.

A second interrogator inside the airport itself questioned the unusual authorization.

He motioned to a superior officer, who came quickly to investigate.

"Do you speak German?" he requested.

RJ responded, "Fluent German, yes."

The superior officer motioned him to proceed.

He boarded the aircraft and found a proper seat by himself. A middle-aged woman came and sat down next to him.

The plane taxied down the runway and into the air.

It appeared that Corporal RJ Smidt had thankfully left France and was headed to Barcelona, Spain.

When the airplane landed in Barcelona they were again interrogated.

This Nazi wanted to know more about his plans in Barcelona. But, to RJ's favor, they were interrupted by two Gestapo agents who were looking for two women.

RJ reached for his papers and moved on to the outside of the building. He was met by a member of the Underground movement in Spain.

The member spoke in German and received his reply in German.

Colonel Barlow Sweet introduced himself to Corporal RJ.

He stated, "I will get you to a train that will bring you to London."

RJ answered, "I haven't heard that name, London, for a very long time."

He drove an American Ford automobile with radio equipment installed on the front dashboard.

The Colonel quickly phoned his people, informing them that he was taking the American to the train station.

Within minutes they had arrived at the large Barcelona train terminal.

He was handed his one-way ticket to London, with one stop indicated.

Corporal RJ thanked the Colonel and saluted him when leaving his vehicle.

In the terminal he found lunch and drinks and boarded the outgoing train headed for London, England.

He was asleep in his seat when a ticket collector announced that they had arrived in downtown London.

Corporal RJ Smidt had returned. He had completed his mission, having done so without harm to himself.

He thanked God and left the train.

There before him was a military counter. He approached the soldier and requested that he call headquarters for him.

The soldier handed the phone over to RJ.

"This is Corporal RJ Smidt. I have completed my mission and have returned to London. I am at the train center in downtown.

"Please send someone down to get me. Thank you."

The soldier offered him a seat to wait for his pick-up.

FIFTY-THREE

SHE RUSHED out of her military auto and into his arms.

"I knew you would make it. I just knew it," she exclaimed, and she gave him a meaningful kiss directly on his lips. She continued, "Now I could possibly get to love you," and she began to laugh.

The corporal returned, "I told you that I had a reason to make it back. Yes, it was for the landlady at my apartment, ha, ha," and he grabbed her torso and gave back a powerful and very meaningful kiss to surprise her.

Major Sandra was lit with excitement. Her man had returned.

He was safe and jubilant. It was to be a great homecoming.

In the eyes of the Allies and his major, he was truly a hero.

For the next several hours she would not let go of him.

She held him tightly and he caressed her neck and hands. Their kisses continued and they spoke of the romantic passion about them.

They needed each other quite desperately and their emotions told it best.

"Please sleep with me tonight," she beckoned.

"Only if you really want me," he responded.

"No, I want the doorman at the pub down the street, ha, ha," she returned.

And so it was. She drove directly to his apartment. They tore into each other, like few do.

For Corporal RJ, Sandra was to be the first woman in his young live.

Major Sandra had once had an affair, when she was quite young.

But they now knew exactly what to do and they did it with devotion and happiness.

Their bodies had never been touched this way, from their heads to their toes. And yes, amazingly they did get some vital sleep.

The morning found them wrapped around each other. Their naked bodies were pressed together.

They knew that he must be returned to headquarters to give them a complete report.

And so, they left his apartment and began the first of many important stops before even reaching headquarters.

The list included a barber shop for a shave and cut and of course some breakfast.

Headquarters would have to wait.

FIFTY-FOUR

HE HAD BEEN living in the French peasant uniform for nearly six days.

Yes, he was able to wash out most of his clothes while in that large room, but what a feeling to get back to a clean and different dress.

He was clean shaven and hair trimmed when he and Sandra arrived at headquarters.

His pressed and cleaned military uniform made him more than presentable.

He and she saluted Colonel Maxwell Barrett and other headquarters staff, as they were escorted into a proper planning room, next to the Colonel's private office.

The group consisted of seven top grade officers, Major Sandra Darling being one of them. Corporal RJ Smidt sat down next to Sandra.

The colonel began, "We welcome you back from your important mission. We congratulate you for succeeding with those important targets.

"Your effort will have saved hundreds, maybe thousands of Allied soldiers and the people, normally in their way.

"We are well aware of the danger you faced each day of the program.

"Our staff has kept me abreast of the many details and logistics involved in your operation.

"You are being promoted for your work to major, effective immediately. You are not to be called corporal anymore. Congratulations once again.

"We are anxious to hear your story, the details and, of course, your experience with the resistance, and later with the underground in Free France.

"Please tell us of your encounter."

Major RJ Smidt began to deliver his long-awaited information.

The details included his bon-voyage, the adventure in the German airplane over Nazi occupied territory, his jump via parachute, his lucky unite with The Resistance, their hide-away, the British soldier, meeting all of this particular group, the welcoming of their supplies, equipment, and attitude towards the new targets delivered to them.

The report on targets, one, two, three, and four, were of great interest to several of the officers present.

He finished with the details of his escaping, including trips to Casablanca, and eventually out of occupied Europe to Barcelona, and finally back to England.

A series of important questions followed his summation. He was able to answer most of them for the inquirers.

The group clapped their hands for the new major's just completed mission.

The colonel called for a recess of fifteen minutes. Coffee, tea, and milk were served along with crackers.

When they sat down again the colonel presented the new major with his uniform pins.

After the commotion calmed down, the colonel made an unexpected announcement.

"Having been thrilled by your actions during the mission, we have decided to make use of your unique skills once again.

"Our staff is working on a program with the Allied Command and you just might be of great help during the planning of an anticipated attempt to retake a portion of France in the very near future.

"We will require you to be present at a meeting in three days.

"They will phone you with information as to day, time, and location. Also, transportation will be sent for you.

"This meeting is adjourned."

Major Sandra was visually unhappy with the announcement.

FIFTY-FIVE

GENERAL DWIGHT Eisenhower called for the meeting for 1300 hours on the second day.

The meeting was scheduled to be in a room under number ten Downing Street in downtown London, adjacent to Prime Minister Winston Churchill's private office.

Security just to get there was extraordinary. To get under number ten was even more so.

Columns of soldiers and military equipment blocked off traffic in all four directions.

Major RJ Smidt and his colonel were the only ones allowed beneath the Hallowed Ground escape location secretly built to house the British government during the war.

Colonel Maxwell Barrett saluted Field-Marshall Bernard Montgomery, General Omar Bradley, and Brigadier-General Clyde Rush, and then introduced his Major RJ Smidt, who quickly added his salute.

They had already heard about RJ's successful mission and were impressed.

The selection for further use of the Major's skills was unanimous.

General Eisenhower was not present at this meeting due to a report of Nazi movement towards portions of Free France.

He had requested the group go ahead with some facets of a major plan that was top secret.

General Bradley began the meeting. "We need someone to help us with very special information prior to our major plans.

"We know that you, with your language skills and veteran experiences, could be the individual that could give us what we need.

"Our staff has been urgently working on this important mission that could have the effect that would possibly shorten the war and ultimately save millions of lives.

"We should be able to get you going on the mission probably in two days.

"Our next meeting will be with General Eisenhower at Southwick in Hampshire tomorrow morning at 0800 hours. Please don't be late.

"Colonel, you and the major may leave now, as we will remain here working with staff on the layout of this important mission."

Major RJ and the Colonel left the building.

The military jeep driver, as a favor, drove the Major to meet up with Sandra at his apartment.

She had been waiting for information and feared more dangerous assignments for her man.

Their second day and night together were even more passionate and romantic than the first day and night.

She cried in his arms, sharing her fears and disappointment. It would have been normal to have had him continue in England for the rest of the war. After all, he had already served this country.

But it appeared that the Allies needed him badly and he was not encouraged to refuse the assignment.

Sandra spoke, "You now know that I love you but couldn't show my feelings before you left on this last mission, concerned that you might not have come back alive.

"But now we must enjoy what time we have left before you leave once again. I will be with you as long as I am allowed to do so.

"Please love me, as much as you can so we can both hold on to the memories until you return, as before."

They kissed and kissed again while shedding their clothes.

The bed springs bounced up and down as they wrapped themselves into sexual positions.

FIFTY-SIX

GENERAL EISENHOWER had just finished having tea.

He welcomed his selected group with his typical broad smile.

They all saluted him and sat down at the pre-arranged conference room.

He began speaking. "You have been called here to help us with our ongoing plans to begin retaking territory currently controlled by the enemy.

"From the beginning, we realized that there could be many different routes to consider before actually developing the plan.

"France is our best target.

"As you know, we have completed 'Operation Torch' which gave victories in Africa. "And we have made appreciable gains in Italy and elsewhere.

"The enemy is expecting our attack to be somewhere along France's coastline.

"They have been fortifying areas from Calais to Normandy and beyond.

"Our secret contacts have not been able to tell us about their fortifications, but we know that they are there and should be of great strength.

"We are prepared to pick one of the areas along the coastline in order to get our personnel and equipment back on French soil to ultimately work our way inland.

"One of our advantages is to keep them from knowing where we will attack.

"We have spies and contacts who will leak out erroneous information to hopefully maintain our surprise.

"This aspect could save a great many lives alone.

"However, we are seeking other methods of helping us during such an attack.

"Our staff has recommended obtaining any last-minute information from the sight that could affect where and when to put our special effort.

"That might mean the difference between winning our mission or not.

"To that end, we have decided that a skilled individual who might get dropped into the French area itself, carrying radio equipment that could contact our leaders just prior to our assault, would be a critical advantage.

"I have been told that you, Major Smidt, have been picked to be that individual.

"We are preparing to train you for the mission thoroughly in the next two days and get you to our chosen area as soon as possible.

"Your mission will include other information that you could find while awaiting the timing of our critical assault.

"The rest of us will be considering the multitude of logistics that will come to this program.

"Our target date will be in four days.

"Any questions will be answered by our staff.

"Thank you for your indulgence and commitment to our goals. I must leave you now for other important meetings."

Everyone arose from their seats and saluted the General, as he departed the room.

Major RJ Smidt now knew what his mission was to entail.

He was anxious to tell Sandra of the basic plan.

Only two days left before leaving for France once again.

Tomorrow will sure to be spent studying and training for the program.

Unfortunately, there will be only limited time with Sandra.

FIFTY-SEVEN

THEY RETURNED to his apartment. She had hugged and squeezed him since they had come together earlier in the afternoon.

Sandra had realized that these few hours remaining with him were so important to her future.

She had confessed to her mother of her genuine love for RJ, and her mother encouraged her to enjoy what is possible now.

When he locked his apartment front door, she grabbed him and began kissing and undressing.

He found his shirt buttons quickly and his chest was quickly bare.

They went at each other like few ever do.

Finally, they made it to the bed. Once in the nude, they embraced and began rolling in the bed itself.

They just couldn't get enough from each other. Their intercourse seemed like heaven to them and it was to be continued for several hours.

She worshipped his manly strength and tender passion.

He carefully stroked her elegant hair and was captured by its beauty. His hands had caressed her breasts and found their protruding nipples.

He kissed every inch of Sandra's body from head to toes.

She would follow without encouragement.

It was true love, and they knew it. They were to be totally positive in their thinking of the future.

RJ asked to marry her, and plan a wedding when he would return.

Sandra was elated and started crying. "Yes," she countered. She added that they should wait until the war was over and just maybe his parents and family, who might have survived the crisis, could come and enjoy it with them.

He began to cry, responding, "Yes, if it were possible, it would make our life together even more meaningful."

They spent the rest of the day and night in his bed.

The next day would be spent learning the detailed plans for his mission.

Sandra would be with him at lunch and dinner, and then to his apartment to make their final love together throughout the night.

Yes, tomorrow is to be an important day for them both.

FIFTY-EIGHT

THEY AWOKE smiling and happy. Sandra led the way to the shower, and they both enjoyed sharing their bodies once again while washing away the residue of the night's actions.

Smartly dressed in their military uniforms they prepared for the day of importance.

They were picked-up by an Army vehicle at 0700 hours as promised.

Once again, they were transported to Southwick in Hampshire.

The bottom floor of the estate possessed several rooms.

One was set aside for training, the others for table planning.

U.S. Army Colonel Ben Collier was assigned to begin training Major RJ Smidt for his mission.

The colonel introduced himself as RJ saluted him.

"Sit down and get comfortable. I will talk first and answer your questions later," he immediately stated.

He continued, "I am about to give you confidential information that has the highest security to it.

"Just a few at the top have been briefed on these decisions and facts.

"The information is to go nowhere, absolutely nowhere.

"If it was to get into the wrong hands, it could affect the lives of millions of soldiers and people. I'm sure you understand.

"General Eisenhower, our supreme commander of Allied Forces, and his closest staff of high-ranking officers, after long considerations, have finally committed our upcoming invasion of France to be on the beaches of Normandy and its surrounding area.

"It is designed to begin our push inwards to free Europe of Nazi occupation.

"The enemy is expecting an invasion, but does not know where or when. "This is an important advantage we must keep.

"Many of our people believe we are going in to Calais. The enemy may also think that to be.

"It is imperative that we keep them guessing.

"To that end, we will send early action as a diversion to several other locations, and to fool the enemy, which brings us to your special mission.

"We are to drop you behind Normandy into the hands of the resistance once again, several days prior to our planned program.

"The resistance will gladly hide you and prepare you to become a Nazi photographer on that invasion day only, who will have access to their defenses along that beach area.

"Your credentials are already being made to give you the special authority to get it accomplished.

"Then, you are to return to the resistance hideout and to radio our awaiting leaders for pertinent information of their defenses that should save our forces valuable time and valuable lives.

"The radio equipment will be sent with you and is not to be used until D-Day, and then only as directed.

"Once we have made occupation of the beach head, the resistance will return you to our Allied Forces. You will have completed your mission for us and are to be sent back to London.

"Basically, you will be our first ally to be 'on the shore at D-Day' without the enemy knowing it.

"You will have a pistol on you throughout your role-playing.

"Hopefully, you will not have to use it to complete your mission.

"Other particulars will be given to you as we get closer to your departure.'

"Are there any questions?"

FIFTY-NINE

THEIR LAST night together was tremendous. They clung together like death was around the corner.

She continually cried and he was emotionally affected as well.

It was still beautiful and romantic in spite of the coming separation.

The transportation arrived. It was 0700 hours as expected.

Major RJ was scheduled to be sent away at darkness.

Sandra would meet up for lunch and to say goodbye before the approaching darkness.

RJ was stripped of his uniform and dressed in French peasant attire once again.

He was packed with some food and water, condensed custom radio equipment strapped to his left leg.

Only a knife was given to him to defend himself if needed, along with the pistol they had previously promised.

He had been taught the complete plans and was aware of the danger involved. RJ knew that if he was caught, he would be killed or tortured.

In his jacket upper pocket was put the official papers that were to be used to photograph the beach area and preparation bunkers at Normandy.

An upscale German camera had been purchased, with proper film, to be used during his walk through the Nazi defense area.

RJ was trained to use the camera and accessories, and now had complete confidence of the usage of the equipment.

The camera and full bag were put into the backpack he was to carry.

Chocolates and gum were loaded into the left-over space in the backpack.

He was ready to go, indeed.

General Eisenhower himself came to say, "Goodbye and good luck."

RJ saluted him and shook his hand.

The importance of his mission became even more evident when the Allied Commander himself had come to wish him luck.

His shortened lunch with Sandra had been without tears.

He had to return for final briefing and they would have their final meal together at about 1800 hours, an hour or so before darkness.

The final briefing included information to be delivered directly to The Resistance.

He was asked to have them target communication lines, just before the assault. It would hopefully stop information being relayed to other parts of occupied France and Germany.

1800 hours had arrived, and Sandra was waiting. They ate Wellington and lightly fried fish for dinner with wine.

Sandra proposed a toast to his successful mission and his safe return to England.

RJ caressed her neck and ears, while finally stealing a major kiss from her lips. They hugged and hugged, talking about their life together. Finally they had ended this last meal together.

She blurted, "I love you so much. Please be safe and come home to me."

He gave her his final kiss.

Sandra let him go.

He was taken by guards to a military building, where he was put into a sedan for the drive to that base near the British Canal, where another captured Nazi airplane was waiting.

SIXTY

THE SEDAN came upon the small airstrip entitled "Peacock," where the stolen Nazi aircraft was hidden.

They rolled it out from the protected brush and readied it for RJ's special mission.

Appearing from the west came Captain Pete Peters and Lieutenant Albert Smithson, the same two who had flown the other craft for RJ in his previous air drop for his last mission.

RJ yelled, "Hey, remember me? You guys got me off to a great start in my last objective. Are you ready for me again?"

The captain answered, "No, we're taking you to Las Vegas, ha, ha."

RJ responded, "Sure, but I hope you guys know the plan. I'm counting on you to do it right."

Lieutenant Smithson came back, "We're ready for your target. Let's go."

They boarded the plane. It was totally dark and wind had died down. The enemy aircraft chugged its way down the strip and into the night.

Nazi shore lights spotted the craft and quickly identified its numbers and swastika boldly displayed.

The plane continued on its low-level flight inland and on to the route to Normandy.

Just before daylight they approached the Normandy area.

Captain Peters located the target point just ahead and alerted RJ to get ready.

Lieutenant Smithson checked and rechecked RJ's parachute and clothing. He was indeed ready to jump.

The bomb gate in the middle of the plane was opened. Two chutes would follow RJ out the gate.

The captain called "Go," and RJ jumped as planned.

Immediately behind him were the other parachutes.

RJ hit the dirt of the field and rolled to his right.

Gathering his chute and releasing his backpack freed him from the fall.

From a hedgerow of bushes came three members of The Resistance.

He had made a successful jump and found his connections.

Boris LaTourne introduced himself and helped him with his gear.

His two other men ran to the landing supplies.

They were put into an old broken wagon, which was being pulled by an old gray horse.

The horse worked its way down the dirt lane and finally stopped at a deserted building that had major damage from this war or the previous war. It was hard to tell.

Boris and his men disembarked and helped him off the wagon.

Under the building was a narrow doorway, which was the entrance to this Resistance hideaway.

He was welcomed by several other individuals, including three women.

They wanted him to relax and enjoy some light food and wine.

He quickly released his radio equipment that had been strapped to his leg.

Boris announced that the supplies had arrived without problem.

RJ was now concerned. In French, he asked them, "Where are these supplies and my special items being stored?"

Boris replied, "Don't worry. We will keep them all right here, in that far corner."

"Great," RJ returned.

He began to enjoy the food and wine, and was introduced to most of the other team in this gathering.

Boris asked, "Could we go over your important material as soon as possible?"

"Yes. I will be able to do so after my thirst is met, which will be in about two minutes," RJ stated.

Boris reached for his second glass of wine.

SIXTY-ONE

THE SUPPLY boxes contained two automatic rifles, ammunition, and hand grenades, plus the upscale German uniform and accessories for RJ's usage.

He had taken with him the authority papers that would hopefully allow him to photograph and inspect the beach defenses along the Normandy coastline.

The papers were forged by British experts, indicating a special assignment from Reich Minister of Propaganda, Joseph Goebbels, with his name scribbled at the bottom of the papers.

Fritz Frugel was RJ's new name with personal credentials to prove it.

The uniform was not usual military dress. This generic uniform had no markings, but it had an armband with the swastika boldly displayed.

He was to carry no weapons, just his given knife and pistol, hidden in his right pants pocket and waistband, respectively.

His actual inspection of the shoreline was to start just before daylight, on the day of the invasion, and not before.

The invasion day could be tomorrow or the next day, etc.

A resistance member worked at the train station control desk. He was to receive a Morse code beep the evening before the planned invasion, which would be relayed immediately to the resistance headquarters, where RJ and others were waiting.

His inspection plan was ready to begin at approximately 0400 hours.

The inspection and photos should be completed within twenty minutes.

He should quickly return to resistance headquarters, where his small radio was prepared to immediately report to several of the generals leading their troops and equipment into battle.

Hopefully the information would be very useful in the invasion strategies employed at the very moments already before them.

This whole group of resistance individuals were aware of what was about to happen.

They were given important requests to eliminate communication lines of the city and involving the military bunkers.

This, too, was to be done early in the morning, just before the invasion itself.

If everything went well, RJ was to be reunited with the Allied Forces, when they began moving inland and not before then.

He would have changed back to his French peasant dress and be ready to hopefully join up with them at that time.

They are to send him back to England as soon as possible.

His mission would hopefully be over.

SIXTY-TWO

THEY WERE waiting impatiently for the signal to reach their contact.

The second day appeared and there was no word at daybreak.

RJ was getting to know the resistance individuals. They were truly committed to doing anything to help get back their country.

The supplies that were sent with him were well received by them. They already had plans to use much of it in future missions.

They also believed that the Allies will win the war, but hopefully sooner than later.

Several of the men had met some of the United States Generals, at meetings prior to the beginning of the war.

Field-Marshall Montgomery had visited much of France also prior to the war, and had shaken hands with two of these resistance members.

They all sat and waited, knowing exactly what their assignments were.

On June 5, at about 1800 hours, a knock on the headquarters' door caught everyone by surprise. It was a messenger from the train station saying, "The code has been delivered," and he quickly left the doorway.

RJ jumped to his feet and clapped his hands, "Yes, I will be going early tomorrow morning, before the sun rises. Hopefully, I should return within thirty minutes or so.

"If something should go wrong, and I don't return within the hour, one of you should set up my radio and attempt to speak to the important generals that need any knowledge that you might have on the defenses that they were about to face when they invade the beaches here in Normandy.

"As you probably know, that is my mission here, to get up to date information about those defenses and relay it to the Allied officers in hopes of saving lives, time, and equipment vital to the success of their mighty invasion.

"If I am fortunate enough to complete my mission, we will be hopeful that our forces get the foot-hole needed to continue their push inland.

"When and if that is established, I should be able to join up with an Ally division and leave you to continue helping the battle. As for now, I am going to try for some sleep before 0400 hours arrives." He began shutting his eyes.

SIXTY-THREE

D-DAY, the sixth of June 1944, was here. The largest organized military operation in modern history was about to take place in the form of an Allied Invasion of occupied Europe on the beaches at Normandy, France.

Their ultimate objective was the liberation of Western Europe from Nazi occupation.

Nearly two days of rain and fog had lifted. It was far from a lovely day ahead of them.

They had already waited one extra day because of the terrible weather. They could not wait any longer.

Over five-thousand ships and landing craft were ready to go.

It was about to be the largest amphibious military assault ever attempted.

Several thousands of soldiers had been parachuted into the villages behind Normandy, hoping to encircle the beachhead and protecting enemy reinforcements from reaching the beach action areas.

Eleven-thousand aircraft were to soften up the enemy and provide protection for the troops.

The invasion targets were to include five beaches.

One hundred fifty-six thousand United States, British, and Canadian fighting men were to be involved in the taking of those five beaches. Daylight was but a few hours ahead.

RJ (or Fritz Frugel) was dressed in his generic military uniform with the swastika armband and carrying his camera case as he entered a large bunker area along the beach.

A guard greeted him, "Who goes here?"

RJ responded, "I am here by authority of Herr Joseph Goebbels. These are my orders and authorization." He handed his credentials to the guard.

"So, what will you do here, and why so early in the AM?" he asked.

RJ returned, "I am to take pictures of you and your men and the fortifications around here for his latest magazines.

"It is to show all of Germany our great defenses and heroic soldiers that guard them.

"I am to continue to do all the beaches by late this afternoon and then fly to Berlin to give the pictures to Herr Goebbels himself. I trust you understand.

"In about fifteen minutes I will leave you and this area and move to another location."

"Yes, I cannot stop you from doing just that. You may go," the guard returned.

RJ started taking his picture and entered the bunker.

Quickly he snapped several interior pictures and left to the beach itself.

He began walking along the lonely sandy beach when he spotted a guard approaching him with his trained dog.

The guard immediately demanded his authorization and identification.

Upon reading them with his trusty flashlight he handed them back to RJ.

"I guess you are okay. Will you take my picture?" he requested.

"Yes, I will see to it that it makes Herr Goebbels's next magazine," RJ returned and he snapped his picture.

"Okay, you may continue on the beach. My dog will not harm you." The guard ended his conversation and began moving in the other direction.

And so, RJ continued on for about a mile or so. He had decided that he had seen enough, and to go back quickly to the resistance hideout.

There were signs of daylight in the far distance.

But Major RJ Smidt had been "On shore at D-Day."

He needed to get to his radio and attempt to reach the commanders of this important invasion before they reached the beaches.

The resistance hideaway was empty. They were out doing their job of cutting off communications as much as possible in the area.

He quickly went to his radio that was available in this basement retreat.

Opening his official papers he began turning the dial to the assigned numbers.

He heard the German language being spoken to a weather unit somewhere in the area.

RJ moved the dial another degree to the left and began speaking into his hand-held microphone.

"General Roosevelt are you there?" he voiced.

Responding, "Just a minute, he is here."

"Okay, this is General Theodore Roosevelt, who is this?" he stated.

RJ returned quickly, "Yes, this is Major RJ Smidt reporting from the beach that you are about to invade.

"Sir, I must tell you that the beachhead is well fortified with cement bunkers, well reinforced.

"Every bunker has seven men, armed with automatic weapons.

"The holes in the bunker walls are but a foot wide and are loaded with updated machine guns of high quality. They seem to have plenty of ammunition.

"The entrances to the bunkers are on your right-hand side when you approach them.

"There are large gun emplacements about every fifty feet, capable of reaching long distances, distances to which I cannot confirm.

"The beaches are planted with land mines and water obstacles.

"Their heavy guns are aimed at the beach area itself.

"There is barbed wire in front of each beach.

"Behind the bunkers are occasional Tiger tanks or other military equipment.

"There are two military buildings about two blocks away from the beach.

"I would guess many soldiers would be in their beds quite early this morning.

"Would you please pass this information to other commands in case I am unable to get to them in time?

"I hope that my information is helpful. May God bless you and our soldiers to victory."

"Roger and out, major. Thank you for the info." The general ended the communication.

(General Theodore Roosevelt was the son of President Theodore "Teddy" Roosevelt, the 26th President of the U.S. and was the Commander of the First US Army, at Utah beach.)

RJ was able to reach three others on his important list when the noise began to block his conversations. The invasion had begun.

He could hear the airplanes up above bombing, and the softening of the beaches from the large military ships' powerful long-distance guns.

Daylight was almost everywhere.

He was glad he had made it back to this safety basement. Still, he could not guarantee his survival even in this location.

He knew he had no choice but to wait here for the Allies to succeed.

SIXTY-FOUR

YES, THERE was a big party waiting for him at headquarters near downtown London. Major Sandra Darling had organized the group of planners and workers involved in putting together this special mission.

The war was not over but an important victory at Normandy had given the Allies the belief that the war could soon be completed.

The two Majors, Sandra and RJ, clung together like never before.

She kissed his face, hands, lips, and neck. His hands were up and down her complete frame, squeezing wherever he could.

They kissed and kissed, madly and romantically, and wouldn't let go of each other.

That first night returning was beyond sex. It had moaning and groaning throughout the hours of bliss at its peak. They climaxed and cried in each other's arms. It continued into the wee hours of the night.

RJ spoke, "Let's get married. I love you and no one else. I want you with me the rest of my life, please."

"Yes, we should. I think I am pregnant with your child already. I missed my period just as you returned. I will go to the doctor's office tomorrow to be sure," she responded.

"Wow," he came back, "I would be thrilled to be a father, and to have you as its mother. I will go with you to see the doctor tomorrow. I couldn't be happier."

Sandra reminded him of her wanting him to attempt to locate his family, in hopes that they might be present at their wedding.

And so, the wedding plans would have to wait until his parents' situation was somehow completed.

Meanwhile, the military announced that they would not send the major on any more missions unless the war changed against the Allies.

They also said that several metals would be given to him at a later date.

French military authorities, those who had luckily escaped capture and were now in England, stated that they would also honor Major RJ Smidt for his bravery and commitment to the helping of their French Resistance.

Major RJ had offered to work with the Allied military planners for the remainder of the war.

They quickly accepted his offer, believing his experiences might just be important in much of the future movements of the conflict.

General Eisenhower had personally agreed to find a space on his staff for his latest hero.

SIXTY-FIVE

WHILE THE ALLIES moved inward from Normandy, the international press caught wind of so many stories about D-Day and began circulating them throughout the free world.

The story about Major RJ Smidt took longer to reach the working press.

It took about three weeks before his story gained attention to the writers of the war.

But, once it was known, it became a headline and front-page story.

The major was labeled, "The first Ally to be on shore at D-Day"

Obviously, his bravery, language abilities, quality training, intelligent decisions, commitment to world peace, and his desire to help stop the notorious thieves and murders of his own Germany brought him to volunteer in England, and to join the military efforts to that end.

Major RJ's personal story became among the best-sellers in most countries.

His efforts saved many lives and equipment, and helped quicken the end of the war in Europe.

The complete details had to be shown in book form.

Thank God, for his survival to tell this story.

SIXTY-SIX

MAJOR RJ SMIDT received his metals from the Allied Forces, The British Army, and from Free France. He was promoted once again, this time to lieutenant-colonel.

Major Sandra exclaimed, "Now you can order me around—militarily, big shot. Ha."

When the war ended, Major Sandra retired from the military with honors, and received a retirement stipend from the British Government for her long and important services.

The new Lieutenant-Colonel Smidt attempted to locate his family.

Unfortunately, his father had been killed by the Nazis.

His younger brother, Boris, had been inducted into the German Army, and was killed fighting in Russia.

His mother had been sent to a concentration camp in Poland, where, by a miracle, she survived.

The United States relocation committee, who had located her, flew her to London to be at the wedding.

Her grandson, named Otto after her departed husband and son, was born soon after the wedding. His mother chose to return to Heidelberg to a sister and friends who had also survived the war.

RJ, Sandra, and Otto stayed in London, but visited his hometown several times before his mother passed on.

When Lieutenant-Colonel RJ Smidt finally left the military, he too received a stipend from the British Government for his unique and special services.

RJ was hired by American Motors, Europe Division, as a Vice President of German Sales & Marketing.

He retired in 2001, and passed away in 2014, at the age of 89.

Sandra Smidt worked for several charitable organizations and died during 2009, at the age of 79.

Their son, Otto Smidt, became the President of Royal-Cluster Premier Belt Company and rose to become a multi-billionaire.

He later was Knighted by the Queen of England, and is now named Sir Otto Smidt.

THE AUTHOR

Burt Jagolinzer has chosen to memorialize his departed relatives that were eliminated by the Nazis during World War II.

He and his local family had lost several uncles and aunts, as well as many cousins, during that terrible period.

This story of Colonel RJ Smidt is certainly an example of the many heroes that came out of the Allies' encounters during that crisis.

May there never be another world war during our lifetime.

Thank you, God.